Anonymous

Wolfern Chace

A chronicle of days that are no more. A novel. Vol. 2

Anonymous

Wolfern Chace
A chronicle of days that are no more. A novel. Vol. 2

ISBN/EAN: 9783337043643

Printed in Europe, USA, Canada, Australia, Japan

Cover: Foto ©Andreas Hilbeck / pixelio.de

More available books at **www.hansebooks.com**

WOLFERN CHACE:

A CHRONICLE OF

"𝔇𝔞𝔶𝔰 𝔱𝔥𝔞𝔱 𝔞𝔯𝔢 𝔑𝔬 𝔐𝔬𝔯𝔢."

A NOVEL,

IN THREE VOLUMES.

BY

One—who not unknown to fame,
Yet dares to write without a name.

Shadows! Oh, ye Shadows that before me pass;
We are all Shadows—Shadows on the grass.
I stand in the bright sunshine, upon this ancient lawn,
And muse in dreamy thought on the Shadows that are gone.

VOL. II.

London:

REMINGTON AND CO.,

5, ARUNDEL STREET, STRAND, W.C.

1879.

WOLFERN CHACE.

CHAPTER I.

CHANGE OF SCENE.

IN a few days, maps and road-books had been gathered and studied; the open-carriage fitted-up with its old-fashioned imperials, from which, with a half-sigh, many a charming dress had been excluded for want of space, or for fear of crushing.

A pair of powerful geldings selected for the start, and another pair sent on, two days in advance, with a careful, steady old groom; and then our family party started on their

travels. Brooks, their light-weight coachman,
occupied the box-seat, Lady Langdale and the
girls the body of the barouche, man and
maid the rumble. Sir Geoffrey and Gilbert
rode chiefly, but occasionally condescended
to take their places in the carriage, whilst
Brooks rode and led their horses. At such
times the box was at a high premium, and the
girls would contest for it as keenly as Tory
and Whig for a seat in Parliament, with the
same hope of " taking the reins."

The roads in those days were enlivened by
many coaches and travelling carriages, and
great carrier's waggons. The posting houses
were all astir with changes of guests and
horses. For a time, however, our travellers
avoided, as much as possible, the larger
bustling thoroughfares, and went by country
lanes and by-roads to Richmond. At this
picturesque point of the Thames they stayed

a few days and with mornings on the river, and afternoon drives to visit old, and almost forgotten, friends, they managed to kill time very agreeably.

Sir Geoffrey had deputed his wife to give Fallington his answer, which she did with all the grace and tact of a fine manner, grafted on a kind heart.

It had been agreed between the parents that he should have leave, on their return, to renew his suit but that, for the present, on the plea of Caroline's shaken health, they could not entertain it. His request to be allowed to join their party at some points of their route had also been firmly, but courteously refused.

Amongst the other revivals of old acquaintanceship at Richmond was one with the Grahames, a poor, but very proud Scotch family, whom the Langdales had for many years endeavoured to retain in their circle, but who, not being in a position to return hospitalities, had resisted so persistently all invitations, that they had been obliged to give them up in despair. This was the more regretted because our friends at the Chace infinitely preferred entertaining guests, to being entertained themselves. They had the harmless vanity of believing that, with very few exceptions, they were more successful, as host and hostess, in putting friends at their perfect ease and comfort, than as guests receiving the attentions of others.

Perhaps a good deal of the art of hospitality turns on that very word—"attentions." Directly visitors are made conscious that they are the objects of forced attentions, they cannot avoid a feeling of uneasiness; a growing consciousness that they themselves are becoming irksome and a source of trouble to their entertainers—and then ? good-bye to all comfort, rest, or refreshment in that house; the sooner the carriage is ordered the better, and the sooner hands are shaken and adieux made, the more hearty and cordial will that hand-shake be.

Some one wrote a clever political treatise on " the art of letting things alone." There is ample room for another treatise on the art of letting people alone, and the key-note of such a treatise would be—" Provide every-thing you can think of as likely to be pleasant to your guests, and then let them alone to enjoy your arrangements."

'Tis simply intolerable to have the mistress of the house, like a fussy old hen, first cluck-ing you along to the drawing-room, and then clucking you away to the library, and murmuring mournfully and anxiously all the while that you are not enjoying yourself. Or

to be trailed about all day by her formal old
peacock of a husband, who stops at every
possible opportunity to spread out his metaphorical tail, in order that you may admire,
and learn by heart, all the glorious spots on
it, and who instantly detects in the incipient
yawn a sign that "you are not enjoying
yourself." Droll! those who first destroy
your enjoyment are the first to feel affronted
at your want of it.

Somewhat of this fussy nature "possessed"
Mrs. Grahame, and it was a blessing to
society that circumstances had prevented
her from often playing the hostess. She was
charming as a guest, because then she did not
feel responsible; but in her own house she was
so anxious for your comfort that she did not
let you have any.

This fussiness simply withered her husband; a proud, sensitive, and somewhat irri-

table man, and hence they were mutally worrying each other through the world and into their respective family vaults much faster than would have been otherwise necessary. I say "respective" family vaults advisedly, for they were so terribly antagonistic to each other in their lives that one felt sure they could not possibly rest peaceably in the same grave. And yet both possessed many good points, which, had they been more fortunately matched, or, perchance, had they had more mutual indulgence for each other's peculiarities, might have developed into fine characters.

His pride was not of the peacockian kind at all, in fact, he was far too proud to be ostentatious. Well-bred, learned, of quick and subtle thought, his sensitiveness would have been a blessing to him as a poet, but as merely a worried married man, goaded to oc-

casional fits of morose madness by the aimless
clacking of this too amiable hen, it was an
unmistakable curse, and the flexible Celtic
temper, with its sparkle of wit and humour,
writhed and hissed under the well-inten-
tioned absurdities to which his wife gave
daily and hourly utterance.

A perfectly miraculous uncongeniality char-
acterised this unlucky couple, and one felt
sure that the Cupid who wickedly bandaged
their eyes, and brought them together must
have worn horns and a tail, and must have
grinned horribly at his own misdeed.

Mrs. Grahame had been the belle of the
season, with an inheritance of beauty, and not
much else, except an affectionate disposition,
and a strong craving for incessant small
martyrdoms and needless self-sacrifices. She
had scarcely a perception of either wit or
humour, so that all her husband's bright

flashes and quaint ideas fell dead upon ears that were open and eager enough for childish small chat, or that would possibly have listened to simple wisdom, if given in patient and loving form.

Finding that she could not, or would not, laugh *with* him, his natural satire was painfully pent in, and at last broke through its prison and laughed *at* her; but, in doing so, it wounded himself, also, like a two-edged sword; for, however much a man may suffer contempt for his wife to take possession of him, it is a contempt that reflects wretchedness on himself.

Now, by a strange freak of Nature, or compensation of Providence, the only daughter, Mary Grahame, inherited the mother's beauty without her silliness, and the father's wit without his acerbity, and this young lady, at the mature age of sixteen, so charmed Lady

Langdale on their first visit to the Grahames that she at once insisted on carrying her off as friend and companion to her two daughters for at least a part of their journey.

Unwise, impulsive Lady Langdale! I presume she forgot for the time that she had a son travelling with them as well as two daughters, or shall we give the dear lady the credit of seeing, with a mother's intuition of character, a future possible bride for her darling Gilbert. I prefer the latter hypothesis, because, although she shared Sir Geoffrey's strong feelings that the husbands of their girls should be equal or superior in wealth and rank to their wives, the logical conclusion of this feeling, of course, pointed in the same direction for the wife of their only son and heir.

Be it how it may, Mr. Gilbert found the unexpected addition to their travelling party a very delightful one. Mary Grahame was so young and almost childlike, both in her appearance and manners, with such a buoyancy of innocent fun in her disposition, that the young gentleman was at first disposed to pet and patronise her, and, indeed, for many days at their halting places, he chiefly amused himself with teasing her into mimic rage, which often ended (amid the hearty laughter of the rest) in something like a wild game at romps. In such-like merry mood they frolicked like young kittens in the funny little " Old Swan" Inn at Thames Ditton, and misbehaved themselves shamefully in the picture galleries of Windsor Castle. Here, however, there really was a fair excuse for some mirth.

An especially pompous custodian had been appointed to take the party round for a private view, and, knowing Sir Geoffrey, was determined to impress so distinguished a visitor

with a due sense of his superiority to the
ordinary guides. Hence he omitted and
aspirated his "h's" in the usual impressive
manner, and with a most exasperating pom-
posity, and, halting his party before one picture, solemnly assured them it " were Venus,
the God of Love, by Polly Titian, a chief of
Dover."

Seeing a merry twinkle in Sir Geoffrey's
eyes, he haughtily corrected his own first
error with a spasmodic, " Goddest, I mean."
Mary Grahame's mischievous grey eyes
literally flashed with fun over the edge of
the cambric handkerchief, with which, in
common with all the other ladies of the party,
she had stifled her mouth, and Gilbert could
not quite suppress a gurgling, half-audible
laugh, which added fuel to the fire. Passing
on thence to a large picture of an apotheosis,
the solemn menial again halted his party,

and, with a majestic wave of the hand, as if he were about to bestow crowns or blessings on everybody, said, in a reverential voice—

" Them is the hangels a carrying off the hinfant princess into 'eaven, and them," with a superior flourish, " and them his the ladies in waitin'."

This was too much for the younger members of the party, who, on various pretexts dispersed themselves to other parts of the gallery to give audible vent to their uncontrollable laughter.

Sir Geoffrey, Lady Langdale, and Caroline covered their retreat as gravely as they could by pretending an especial interest in the next few pictures, but Offended Dignity marched them through the remaining galleries in contemptuous silence.

On issuing from the Castle gates they heard loud sounds of music close at hand,

and suddenly found themselves involuntarily placed at the head of a column of very drummy and trumpety "Odd Fellows" or "Loyal Buffaloes," or some other bedizened Brotherhood, marching statelily along, as if the welfare of the realm depended upon their flaunting banners, flowery aprons, gaudy sashes, and sham stars-and-garters. These gallant Brethren of their Order were fringed on each side by ragged edges of dirty little shouting boys; slouchy, disreputable hob-a-de-hoys and draggle-tail girls, all more or less delirious with delight at the spectacle of Jones, Brown, Robinson and Smith walking four abreast, in fine clothes, and otherwise, making fools of themselves.

To escape contact with this unsavoury fringe, which, like "coming events," cast their (odours) before them, our travellers had to march patiently in front of the motley mas-

queraders—not being particularly gratified at
the probability of being mistaken, by the good
people of Windsor, for an integral part of
this Tomfoolery. If the young members had
been alone it is tolerably certain that they
would ingloriously have taken to their heels
to escape the propinquity, but a party of six,
amongst whom were a dignified lady and a
middle-aged Baronet, to do so was a proceed-
ing not to be thought of; hence, with mingled amusement and annoyance, they were
thus escorted to their hotel, and the whole
affair served them with more matter for
mirth during the sequent lunch, for which
meal it had by no means deprived them of
appetite.

Happy age when youth and pleasure flash
gaiety from bright eyes to brighter, and send
the light ringing peals of musical laughter
echoing through hearts that have never

yet been dulled by sorrow and deadened by care !

Mild *bon-mots*, an indifferent paradox, or the trifling drolleries of custom and character, suffice *then* to make up the gay, light comedy of life for the easily-pleased spectators. " All the world's a stage, and all the men and women merely players " had never seemed so vividly true to the younger folk as now, when the scenes shifted with each passing hour, and a bustling succession of ever new actors passed and repassed before them at every halting-place; and then, (all unconsciously) they, too, were acting a part.   Gilbert was imperceptibly beginning to rehearse his as the Lover (his first appearance in that cha-racter).

Happily however, it was young love— light-comedy love—not the serious, melo-dramatic business; so whilst it doubled his enjoyment of everything in the world, it had not, as yet, a heartache with it. If this sweet, innocent delight of two young hearts in their first mutual attraction and sympathies could but last, what a brave world this would be, my masters!

'Twas that made the fresh fragrance of the early morning—its soft light, its quiet and coolness, so delicious to Gilbert, as, rising with the sun, he took his plunge in the bright river, and then, with renewed vigour in his arms, sent his light wherry flying over the placid stream.

'Twas that that made the meeting at breakfast-time so bright and happy, and the pushing on to "fresh scenes and pastures new," so full of interest and expectation; and, if truth must out, 'twas that, also, made his gallant horse so much fuller of fire than Sir Geoffrey's, and so much addicted to trying his stride over wayside hedges and rails; especially when the travelling carriage came up alongside the horsemen.

Aha! good Soldan, are you also in love without knowing it? and are you really anxious to show how gracefully you can do the demivolt, and how easily you can top a fence to win a smile from Mary Grahame's beautiful lips and kindling eyes?

No! I incline to think that, left to yourself, you would be quite content to settle down, pace for pace, with your steady stable-companion; but there are (or were) some tempting turf-verges on the pleasant road into Henley; broad, springy and elastic; and a young fellow like Gilbert must have been more than mortal if he had resisted the temptation of trying to "witch the 'world' with noble horsemanship," the said world being, of course, only that rather limited, but very delightful little bit of the planet which came within the easy range of vision of a pair of sparkling, mischievous eyes.

It is pleasant to recal, when one is old and apt to be grumpy and discontented with our much-abused planet, how very small a space upon it will amply suffice for intense enjoyment, when that space is fully and brightly illuminated by Love; and also, what very trifling—indeed, quite childish, incidents fill up the measure of that enjoyment, until it overflows with its own gladness, when the same delightful magic touches us with its glamour.

Then, even the *désagremens* of travel are delightful, and a circumstance that would have embittered Mr. and Mrs. Crabapple's lives for a whole day is merely laughed at and hailed as " fun" by the bright young Princess Golden Locks and the gay Prince Graceful.

Thus it chanced at Henley, the large hotel
being full, our travellers were relegated to a
humble little whitewashed hostel on the far
side of the bridge, but "oh, what dear, delightful, funny little rooms," and oh, how
nice the river looks from the droll little
window, and what a clean, tidy, good-
tempered landlady; and the dinner, so simple,
but so charmingly sent up, and such delicious
cream, and eggs, and tea, and " really not
bad wine," chimes in the Prince, " and the
home-brewed, capital."

"Yes, yes, all very charming, no doubt;
but come again, young people, say thirty
years hence, and then—" Bah! what a dirty
pot-house kind of inn—smells of smoke and
beer frightfully. Nothing to eat but boiled
eels and chops like leather. Wine, oh!
poison. Tea, rubbish, broomsticks! Cream,

milk bewitched !" Yes, then it is that the milk
of human kindness is indeed " bewitched "
and our Mr. and Mrs. Crabapple, aforesaid,
turn everything sour by their own acidity.
Happily there was not even the most distant
relationship to Mr. and Mrs. Crabapple in
the whole party. Sir Geoffrey enjoyed his
much-needed respite from many labours with
a thankful heart, and felt as if a heavy weight
had been suddenly lifted off his shoulders;
so that very soon, some of the buoyancy of
youth began to show itself once more, and
he half forgot his age. To Lady Langdale
it was a delightful rest from the cares and
anxieties of a large establishment, which
in their recent pressure had put too great a
strain upon her, in many ways; for who does
not know how constant and wearing is the
mental fatigue of ruling and guiding the wills

of half-educated minds, and soothing and re-
straining their hasty, half-childish tempers
and passions ?

It has been well said that we must learn
to govern ourselves before we can fitly
govern others, but the first task is child's
play compared to the second. To a clear
head and a controlled temper how vexatiously
illogical, and how distressingly violent all the
domestic storms in tea-pots are that perennially agitate, into temporary insanity, the
various Jacks and Jills of a large household.
There is perhaps not a single country house
or town mansion in the whole of merry (but
pugnacious) England that is not periodically
shaken to its centre by fearful internecine
war amongst the domestics. A civil war in
one sense, but a most unmistakably uncivil
war in another. Feuds as bitter, whilst they
last, as those of Highland clans or Kilkenny

cats, with a comic kaleidoscopic shifting of parts and parties that would be highly amusing if it were not so dreadfully inconvenient. Sometimes for a month or week, a day or hour, the squabble will be (as the lawyers would put it), Bailiff and Henwife *v.* Gardener and Cook, and a fight between the men will seem imminent, whilst " evil-speaking, lying and slandering" will be freely exchanged between the pending parties to the suit. Well, the master and mistress of the house compose this feud into a sullen truce, and a short armistice ensues ; when lo, the fire breaks out in a quite new and unexpected place. Now 'tis bailiff and wife aided by gardener and cook (the late sworn foes) who have patched up a fervent alliance, and are wildly irate with the butler, who outnumbered, makes a masterly retreat to the wine-cellar, and there defends and consoles himself; then coachman and James come to the rescue, probably with a keen eye to future bottles of brandy, and a sortie is made, the outsiders are driven back, and the cook forced to capitulate in his own kitchen. Peace is once more restored and doubtless cemented by cognac. Then comes "a little war;" little, but very shrill and virulent, between the laundry-maids and nurses; the housemaids and page take sides, and the pibroch skirls wildly from basement to attic, and from house to laundry, until the dairy also is roused, and its presiding Minerva joins in the small homeric fray.

The "evil-speaking, lying and slander-ing" in this lesser war is not quite so ponderous and astounding, but the vitupe-rate energy is exquisitely acute; indeed a great many tones too sharp for delicate ears. The grander belligerents look on with some-

thing of contemptuous pity at this " woman's
war," which ends generally as abruptly as it
began, in tea and tears, whilst the page is
rightly-served, like the convenient cat, by
being kicked out for putting his nose into
such matters; indeed, like an unsuccessful candidate for Parliament, he is rejected
by a large majority.

Of course one can understand that a temporary escape from all these absurdities (which
are the more trying because absurd) was infinite refreshment to Lady Langdale, whilst
Caroline's relief from the wearisome chatter of
Mr. Fallington was a large element in such
enjoyment as was possible to her in her present state of feeling. To Mildred, heart-whole,
and therefore joyous as a child, everything
was new and delightful, to her indeed—

> " The world was young and beautiful,
> For Fancy dwelt with Truth."

To Mary Grahame, released from a home of painful and distressing strife, which even her sunny nature and quiet tact could not do more than soothe into occasional sullenness, such a change as this was like the escape of Proserpine from Hades.

As for Gilbert, he would indeed have been hard to please, if with such a party, and such a Proserpine, he had not been as happy as the day was long. A powerful " thorough-bred " bounding under him, with nothing to carry but youth, health and high spirits—a seat on the box, and a laughing chat with the girls when tired of the saddle, and quieter but still pleasant talk with Sir Geoffrey, as they rode side by side on the turfy margins of the hedge-bordered, well-kept English roads and lanes, were further integers in the sum of his then pleasure. Poor boy, he was

probably nearer the metaphorical seventh
heaven then, than ever before or since.

At Henley they rested their teams for a few
days, and pulled down stream through that
charming part of the Thames by Marlow to
Cookham and Cliefden. Here, at Cookham,
they found what the girls called a "little love"
of a fishing Inn, from the windows of which
they could drop a line into the stream or chat
with Gilbert as he paddled his boat about before breakfast. Sir Geoffrey, like Gilbert, was
an early riser, and had an intense enjoyment of
the sweet, calm hush of the early morning—
the delicious fragrance of the fields, the cool
refreshment of the dew-softened air ; the
rejoicing life of birds and bright winged in-
sects, the flashing of the silvery fish, and the
soothing, rippling flow of the majestic river.

The motley primitive life of the nomad

tribes " who live and move and have their
being " in barges, was also a source of interest
and amusement to him; and as he sat at the
window, lazily pretending to read or write,
but really only observing and dreamily
thinking, he would often let his thoughts stray
into the odd ways of the dwellers on the
river as they passed in their slow-moving
barges up or down stream, or anchored for a
time under the windows.

Long before the villagers were astir, these
modern Noahs, with their wives and their
children, would emerge from their little cabins,
first a bright comely young woman with the
freshness of the early morning in her face
and the sunshine in her eyes, would carefully
lift up on to the tiny deck of the barge, a
pet bird in a cage, and put a cup of water
for his bath; then a demure and well-trained
cat would leap lightly on deck, and, warned

by the up-raised finger, betake itself out of temptation to a warm dry corner, which had been touched by the first sun-rays; then a merry, barking little dog, almost wagging its tail off with delight; then a rosy, flaxen, curly-pated baby was brought into the sunshine, and its noisy manifestations of a vigorous appetite were soothed and gratified in the usual motherly way; finally the placid husband and father came forth, slowly finishing his previous demi-toilette. A pail of water served alike for laver and looking glass; a pair of brawny hands for face-washers, and a piece of squared fabric (very suggestive of sail cloth) for towel. This sacrifice to the Graces completed, a pannikin of tea and hunks of bread and pork were discussed with infinite relish. After which the barge was slowly pushed off into the stream, and barge, wife, dog, cat and bird,

slowly passed away into space, leaving nought
but a whiff of tobacco smoke from Mr. B.'s
pipe behind.

" What a contrast," said Sir Geoffrey,
when describing this little scene at breakfast,
" to the life of the Hon. Mr. Rushabout, the
Tory whip. Think of these people, placidly
streaming down, slowly hauling up, to and
from a London wharf to Oxford, past sleepy
old towns and villages, for ever and for
ever, like the swing of a long pendulum."

" The swing of the pendulum is sometimes disagreeably interrupted by the swing
of the tide, sir," said Gilbert, " and then your
placid friend is given to using rather strong
language. Of all classes of His Majesty's
subjects, I do not know a more surly,
irascible set of men than bargees, nor a more
sulky, misanthropic race, than the lock-men."

" Easily accounted for, dear boy. 'Evil

communications corrupt good manners,' and these two classes have very little communication with any of their fellow beings except the members of the University of Oxford."

" Thank you, good sir, I'll owe you one, as Dr. Pangloss would say; but to head back to your contrast : would you rather be Mr. Rushabout or a barge man ? "

" H'm, the difference between a penny cracker and a tadpole ! A painful choice if one had to make it ! The one man all flash and bang and fire and smoke, going through life in a series of galvanized jumps, bursting up at spasmodic intervals, and ending in a few bits of blackened paper; the other, a watery, ambiguous monster that it would be simply mockery to call a " man " at all. The animal eats, and drinks, and sleeps, and " tadpoles " itself up and down the river for

a given number of years, and is in due time
sculled across the Stygian stream by a
grimmer and grimier Charon than himself."

" Well, yes; I suppose his sole idea of
Elysium would be innumerable riverside
"publics" in which limitless pots of porter
were to be had without chalking up a score;
and in which he and his mates might sit in a
perpetual cloud of tobacco smoke."

" I wonder what these men did before
Raleigh brought tobacco into this country ?"
said Lady Langdale.

" Why, just a little while before that
time they amused themselves by smok-
ing and burning heretics, and the previous civil wars had provided them with
a great many burnt and smoked towns
and villages.   Perhaps, but for the narcotic
influence of the much abused and still more
used 'weed,' they might retain enough of

that fine old English fierceness to smoke us."

"Smoke us, papa! What do you mean?"

"I mean, smoke us out of house and home, as some of these enterprising gentry have recently served poor Dr. Priestley in Birmingham."

"What a shame!" said Caroline, probably with a vague, uneasy fear that Pierce might some day share the same fate. "And what a cruel return to make to one who was endeavouring to enlighten the ignorant."

"Poetical justice, dear Carrie," said Gilbert; "he was bringing down the light of knowledge to the mob, and the mob illuminated him with the light of ignorance."

"It is too bad of you, sir, to make light of such a heavy loss," said Mary Grahame. "You deserve to be burnt as a heretic."

"No, thank you, Miss Grahame; I prefer a milder flame—besides, to burn one heretic in half a century is now considered a sufficient profession of faith, so they will not need to burn me."

"Well, it certainly was a burning shame," said Mildred.

"Oh! oh! my Lady the Countess, are you adding fuel to the fire of discord?" said Sir Geoffrey. "I wonder that so mild a young lady should grow red with rage."

"I shall be in a rage with you, papa, if you make such bad puns on my good name—remember, sir, 'he who filcheth from me my good name,' etc., etc. Please finish the quotation for me, Mary."

"There's no need for Miss Grahame to trouble herself, my little Belle Sauvage; I did not take your name in vain; I merely divided it, and gave you the two halves—

besides, if I had taken it, remember, it was I who first gave you that name."

" When I was very young I used always to think that 'M' or 'N' had given me my name," said Mary Grahame.

" Did that give you any desire to change it, Miss Grahame?" enquired Gilbert, significantly.

" No, sir, it did not—my name is such a pretty one, that it will take a very strong inducement indeed to change it," retorted Mary, with just the least little bit of a flush and a frown.

" What ages ago, dear Mary, it must have been since you were very young," laughingly said Lady Langdale, " you are such a very ancient person now."

" Quite wrinkled," said Gilbert.

" Careworn," added Mildred.

" Grey-haired," said Caroline.

"Toothless," said Sir Geoffrey.

In answer to these last aspersions, Mary shook her flowing silken hair, and smilingly showed a set of dainty little pearls, and, with mock indignation, threatened dire revenge on all her slanderers and persecutors.

"I'll—I'll—" she began.

"Try a little more cream," interrupted Sir Geoffrey.

"I'll—I'll—

"Have a little honey, dear," said Mildred.

"I'll—I'll—"

"Try some toast, my love," put in Carrie.

"I'll—I'll—"

"Kiss and make it up—not excluding any of the offenders from pardon," said Gilbert.

With such like sunny bubbles, "trifles light as air" on the stream of their sunny life, they beguiled Time of his hour-glass, and added feathers to his wings. Surely

the old man with his scythe had some
compunction in cutting down such bright
little wild flowers for, you see, he picked a
few of the poor little half-withered things,
and laid them in the cabinets of kindly
memory. But the ceaseless, remorseless
scythe goes solemnly, silently on, whether we
wake, or sleep, or laugh, or mourn—sweeping
down the minutes and the hours days,
weeks, years, centuries, until the great
Harvest of Human Life is all cut down and
withered.

Meantime, *vive la bagatelle !* was the order
of their day, and in this spirit they returned
up river to Henley, and thence by road to
Oxford.

At Oxford Mr. Gilbert felt himself quite at
home ; and with a latent pride, smothered
under a deal of flimsy humility, and an eager
exultation, very indifferently cloaked by

nonchalance, entertained the party right-
royally in his rooms. He had written on to
his knowing Gyp and housekeeper to get
everything in splendid order for the ladies,
and to set out all his prizes, and challenge-
cups, and other glories in their full grandeur.

But to Lady Langdale's intense amusement, he had ordered in about a bushel of
dainty biscuits of every possible description
and four or five kinds of wine for their first
early refection, after a luxurious breakfast at
the "Angel." The girls, of course, were too
busy ransacking his rooms to care for wine
and biscuits, and, hence, with a dawning perception of the absurdity of this early lunch,
he hurried his party out to the Bodleian, and
left them there whilst he held long and
earnest consultation with his myrmidons on
the important subject of dinner. Here he
was more at home, and the sight-seers, bring-

ing back with them wonderful appetites,
after their exhausting labours, the dinner was
a great success. Gilbert began to think how
very charming it would be to have a Mrs.
Gilbert Langdale to dine with him every day,
and help to entertain his guests so gaily as
Mary Grahame did. Indeed, these two
young people, aided by Mildred, were the
life of the little party that day, for Lady
Langdale was really fatigued; Caroline could,
of course, only be expected to show a forced
cheerfulness, and Sir Geoffrey was distrait and
anxious, having just received terrible news
from his lawyer, involving, indeed, no less
a stake than the loss of his entire property.

With the best and highest intentions in
the world, he had embarked a large part
of his wealth in an undertaking, which
besides having a fair and reasonable probability of success as a " venture," had, what

was a still greater attraction to him, namely,
a large national benefit as its leading aim.
Some rascally charlatans and hypocrites,
trading under the cloak of philanthropy, had
cunningly wormed themselves into the very
heart of the enterprise, and there living,
thriving and fattening, they gradually ate
and ate it all away, and left nothing but a
hollow, worm-eaten stem, with a fair outside
of bark to conceal its decay. A rough chance
blow revealed the hollowness, and down fell
the goodly-seeming tree with a crash that
made " ruin " echo far and wide through the
land.

" Ruin!" four letters glibly spoken—swiftly
written, but what a " mort" of meaning in
them. Ruin ! Oh, most prosperous sir,
most dainty madam, have you ever had those
four letters staring at you hard in the crabbed
handwriting of a lawyer's clerk ? A very ugly

stare I can assure you; and painfully suggestive of the Gorgon's eyes, whose amiable
peculiarity it was to turn the heart to stone,
and blanch the cheek by their pertinacity.
And oh! most smug, most pious, oily "pro-
moters!" sleek, sly worms, in the shiniest of
hats and boots, and the most irreproachable
black coats and trousers—some day—soon, a
gentleman in, perhaps, still glossier black,
with just a *soupcon* of recently burnt brim-
stone on his flame-coloured handkerchief (instead of your favourite eau de Cologne), will
give you a pleasant, but rather a long and
eventful, journey on a thinnish broomstick;
and take you through the length and breadth
of this, and other lands, so that you may con-
template and enjoy the results of your
financial skill.

Well, yes—he will probably begin with
the city; and lifting the roof off a garret, he

will point out, with an emphatic finger, and
with a hot, wicked leer in his red eye—a
seamstress working eighteen hours of the
day and night to obtain the splendid stipend
of 8d. from Messrs. Shiney and Slops, the
great outfitters.   You will observe, this
specimen of humanity is thin, sunken-eyed,
hollow-cheeked, with garments nearly as thin
as her body, which show her bones, through
both skin and garment, with rather a painful distinctness; but, if you examine carefully the sole ornament of the room, a frame-
less miniature, by the flickering light of the
candle-end by which she is straining her eyes,
you will see what she was once like; a maiden
lady, left with a modest, but sufficient com-
petence, until tempted by your glowing
prospectus of the Flash and Credit Bank, to
invest it in shares in that short-lived, apo-
plectic enterprise.   Yes; look well round and

enjoy the full results of your skill in feather-
ing your own nest so comfortably out of that
affair; contrast, you know, is a great element of enjoyment. Curtains? Well, no;
not quite equal to your damask-silk hangings
—but a broad daily paper pinned against the
window is useful and ingenious. Bedding?
hum!—straw—wholesome, if it were not
quite so dirty. Furniture? Item, one ricketty
small deal table on three legs, and one ditto
chair; both in use. No! no superfluous
luxuries there! scarcely worth a broker's
while to seize for rent; perhaps you would
like to spare a few of your superfluous chairs
and tables. Yes! Ah, but you're "too late"
my friend—you've got nothing now yourself
except this broomstick; and, the honour of
my society for an indefinite period.

But come, I see the air of this garret is
beginning to disagree with you—we'll go to a

country parsonage and see what you have done to benefit the clergy. Scarce need to lift the roof off the parsonage, one can peer easily through the broken windows—and there you will see a white-haired venerable man, leaning his head on his hands in an attitude of utter despair and prostration of spirit; his aged wife, with trembling hands and streaming eyes, vainly striving to read a letter. You recognise the documents—yes, quite right; 'tis your own clever, plausible explanation of why the Noodle-cum-Diddle silver mine had so rapidly collapsed. Pretty tableau, isn't it?

The grandchildren, you see, have gathered round with wistful eyes wondering what it all means—they have been *hungry* before—but now they must *starve*. Let me see—you purchased your snug estate in Bedfordshire soon after that collapse—wouldn't you like to give these poor folks the use of the house for a time—yes?

"Too late—too late." Your hopeful son has already gambled it away. But quick, hey-*presto*, mount your broomstick again, my oily friend; we have to look in at a certain deserted manor house, where you were often (too often) hospitably entertained. You remember well the generous open-hearted, unsuspicious host, with his warm and kindling sympathies for every good cause, and every worthy enterprise. You remember how chucklingly you took advantage of this weakness to entangle him in your plausible scheme for the reclamation of "No Man's Land," and the rescue of its inhabitants from starvation. You remember what a bright home this was, with its kind and gentle lady-hostess, and the happy children, and ever-welcome guests. Look,.

'tis quiet enough now— it sleeps heavily
and darkly in the midst of its dank, deserted
gardens ; no lights from its dingy, blear-
eyed windows, no flash of fire or mirth in its
halls or chambers—'tis paying a gloomy pen-
ance for its once gaiety. The toad and the
snake crawl and glide about the doorways
without fear of being trodden on by their
human imitators, and the owl hoots its satisfaction at the decay, no longer mimicked by the
featherless biped who caused it. Yes, "thou art
the man!" To-morrow night you shall dig deep
in the churchyard, and see the gentle lady in
her grave—after her pauper's funeral—then
to the asylum and workhouse to watch the
happy children—and to the county jail to
visit your ruined "friend." You don't wish
to trouble me ? No trouble in the world! I
rather like it, because you evidently enjoy
these scenes so heartily, and there are

thousands upon thousands of folk whom you
never knew for whom you were skilful
enough to prepare little simple pleasures
and surprises of this kind in various degrees ;
you will have ample time to study them
deeply, and to pay repeated visits to each and
all. Yes, it might be instructive for you to
spend a few hundred years in a similar garret
to that occupied by your friend the seamstress ;
and another period in the roofless parsonage,
with that interesting tableau engraved on
steel on the walls—and a third cycle in the
deserted manor house, crawling with the toad
and the snake, hooting with the owl, and
gibbering with the bodiless inhabitants of
" No Man's Land."

* * * * *

Some such plausible scoundrel as Mephistopheles was thus carrying about on the thin

broomstick, had indeed been the chief agent in this sudden and overwhelming ruin; for in those days not even the partial protection of the limitation of risk existed for those who embarked in public ventures. The news came with a harsher shock upon poor Sir Geoffrey, inasmuch as the ill-tidings arrived just as they were sitting down to his son's little dinner.

How often there seems an ugly fatality in such matters!

Since the time of Belshazzar's feast, I wonder how many times the handwriting has appeared on the wall to scare us in the very midst of our little mortal pleasures? Sometimes the ill-news hits us, like an arrow, just when we are soaring up for a little while above the cares of office and home. Sometimes it comes as the climax to a long series of physical pains and mental worry, like the last messenger that came to Job.

Come how it might, it could not fail to make Sir Geoffrey clouded, silent and absent, but he put a great strain on himself, and shook off the horrid nightmare with as cheerful a courage as a man could possibly show. His chief forecast, of grief, his bitterest heart-sickness, was not for himself, but for his wife and children; therefore he crushed the letter in his hand, and spake no word concerning it; wisely considering that it would be mere cruelty to give them this pain even a day sooner than need was. Besides, he fairly reasoned that this was but threat of ruin after all, and that the end was not yet; that it might be averted, or at least partially avoided, and therefore " sufficient unto the day was the evil thereof."

So far, wisely and kindly; but in continuing

the journey, as if nothing had happened,
he was not equally wise; but it was the
wrong of a too kind heart, that ached at
the thought of abridging the enjoyment of
those he loved so dearly. For himself, the
remainder of that pleasure trip was a misery
and a mockery. The thread-suspended
sword was ever over his head, the clouds
were on the horizon through the sunniest
days, food was as tasteless as bran, and
wine, bitter in the mouth and hot in the
brain. The overflowing gaiety and light
talk and laughter sounded in his ears as if
afar off—echoing back out of a lost land of
half-forgotten happiness.

Lady Langdale and Caroline both saw that
some great strain was at work in Sir Geoffrey,
and often interchanged whispered fears and
wondering anxieties as to what it might be;
but to the younger trio, two of whom were

being slowly blinded by love, his forced cheerfulness passed current as real.

By easy stages, they had now arrived in the Black Country, and Sir Geoffrey, wishing Gilbert to see life in its varied phases, took him a night journey on one of the barges that ply on the canals through the very heart of that strange land. A wild and weird panorama this unveiled; they glided under tunnels of a darkness so palpable, so intense, that it seemed as if they were cleaving through solid black marble; and then, as they silently emerged from these tunnels, vast cavernous foundries, glowing with blinding light and heat, were revealed on either hand close to the banks of the dark water. These caves of Vulcan being quite open on the water side, all that was being enacted in them could be seen as if it were a drama; and a mad drama enough it looked.

The roar and glare of the furnaces, the
streams of red and white-hot metal, the
deafening clank of the hammers and anvils,
the fantastic spray of brilliant sparks, and the
straining and striving figures of the strange
beings, who seemed as if they were fighting
for the golden-bright masses that were flung
to them,—made up a midnight picture
strongly suggestive of a still hotter and more
terrible scene.   The heat was so intense
that these sons of Tubal-Cain were as scantily
clad as their great progenitor, and their bared
grimy arms and legs, and massive brawny
chests glistened and gleamed in the unearthly
glare as if they were moving and struggling
in an atmosphere of fire. Their hard-featured,
strongly   marked   visages,   set   into   an
expression of almost savage earnestness,
were revealed so vividly by the light, that
they looked like statues of red-hot bronze.

Hoarse shouts of warning and stern commands rang out high above the roar and clank, and at each such shout the wild fight with the subtle demon, "Fire," seemed to re-commence.

To Gilbert all this was simply a curious glimpse into a new condition of human existence, but to Sir Geoffrey it seemed like a nightmare; the gliding slowly down through these strange scenes of life into the blackness of darkness, and emerging upon fiery ordeals on either hand, was too cruelly typical of his own present and probable future, and his overwrought brain could hardly repress the fantasy that he had already passed into Hades.

"What a life," said Gilbert. "Could it be worth while to live at all, to live thus?"

"To us—no! But these, who have known no better, doubtless have their rough compensations for their rough toil."

"I can hardly conceive how."

"Why, of course, it is difficult to strip ourselves, in thought, from all the adjuncts of our own special position—to come out of our own bodies, in fact, and inhabit those of others; and yet until we force imagination to do so, we can form no real or adequate estimate of the possibilities of such other life."

"Let us try," said Gilbert. "Suppose you and I had been a father and son, born in this black region of noise and flame and stifling smoke, and that it was our destiny to earn our bread by wrestling, day after day, and night after night, with the ponderous inertias of Nature, through what avenues of such an existence could any sort of happiness reach us?"

"Animal natures have animal pleasures. The mere eating and drinking, which to us seems often a weary necessity, wasting time

that we crave for other purposes, to such men
is an intense enjoyment. When we are out
hunting, say for seven or eight hours in the
saddle, on a cold, raw February day, without
so much as a glass of sherry or a biscuit,
what a fine sauce hunger makes for the
homeliest dinner. Up a mountain, or over
the stubbles for a long morning's tramp,
when the scouts have mistaken the rendez-
vous, there's a strong satisfaction in seizing
the first hunk of bread and cheese, or
anything else that comes handiest. This
pleasure which, with us, is only occasional, is,
beyond all doubt, a daily one to the hard-
worker."

" A daily pleasure in his daily bread—yes;
that scores one point for the ungentle life."

" Well, then, they do not all beat their
wives, and even those who do, probably derive
a grim satisfaction from the process, until

impertinently interfered with by the law;
whilst those who do not, take an honest pride
in their own good nature, and often evidence
a simple-hearted, rough-and-ready affection
for their belongings, none the less strong and
sincere for its roughness."

" Beating the weak and defenceless can, I
hope, be only a very transient pleasure, like
other acquired tastes."

" I hope not; but in savage natures it
scores for something, or it would not be done.
Then for amusements, have they not the
ever-present pipe and the pet bull-dog; their
rat-killing, drinking bouts, and cock-fighting;
culminating sometimes in the highest excitement of all—a prize-fight amongst themselves ? "

" Yes; I suppose they really do, like the
old Homeric warriors, 'drink delight of battle
with their peers.' "

" Especially when they have previously drunk another kind of delight first."

" But now for their work ? "

" Well, we must confess it does not look inviting at first sight; and yet I can conceive a strong man's pleasure in putting forth and showing his strength; a stirring sense of savage exultation at being able to lift more or strike harder than another; and all down the scale of muscular power each man can have that cheap satisfaction, except the weakest of all."

" Rather hard for this last."

" Yes; but even he can be a Hector amongst the boys, or, perhaps, these are the men who, being beaten by everybody else, find their homely consolation in wife-beating."

" Except for such brutalities which, let us hope, are rarer than they seem, the rough life is not so intensely dreadful as it first seemed."

" On the contrary, I believe it—or a few degrees above it—say that of the skilled artisan class—has more possibilities of sound and sensible happiness than black-coated 'shabby gentility.' Aye, I will even go further, and say that few conditions of life offer a better chance for making a really happy home."

" But then a man must have been born and bred to it."

"Of course; one does not take a race-horse and put him in the plough—he would chafe himself to death. And yet strong and slow, well-fed, quietly-worked Dobbin has a much happier life than the Flying Dutchman, and does not go to the dogs with anything like the same rapidity."

" Ah, but I'd rather be the racehorse ! "

"Doubtless; but that does not diminish Dobbin's placid happiness! but this horsey simile is hardly fair to our friend the artizan, who is not confined to a plough-track, and who has many sources of intelligent enjoyment, and possibilities of high intellectual, as well as manual, excellence, even in his daily work."

"It is certainly a more manly career than that of a man-milliner."

"Aye, and a more suggestive one; you know well enough that most of our great discoverers have been men of that class. Then look at the sons of an artizan; what a much happier life is theirs than that of the mere schoolboy. The latter has a mass of word-knowledge drummed into his unlucky little brains, years before he can either understand or digest it. The process is eminently repulsive to him, whilst being enforced, and,

more or less, useless, to him through the rest
of his life. The boy of an artizan gets his
three R's, and if he is naturally capable of
more, acquires it for himself; and self-acquired
knowledge is worth ten times as much as
'cram.' Meanwhile, almost as soon as he
can walk, hands and head are alike being imperceptibly educated by helping 'father' to
use things, instead of words. See with what
pride a little urchin, only just breeched, files
a rod of iron, or saws a piece of wood, or
deftly drives a nail, whilst young Lord Tom-
Noddy is being mercilessly caned for not
understanding the impossible."

"Ah, I have a very vivid recollection of
these 'pleasures of learning' in my own case,
and remember feeling the bitterness of the in-
justice, even more than the smart of the cane."

"You see there are underlying compensations in every form of life, and no form is

probably anything like so terrible as it may appear to the onlooker."

Sir Geoffrey had instinctively fallen into the train of thought indicated by this chat with Gilbert, and for some little while longer he managed to bear the strain of a seeming cheerfulness under a crushing anxiety; but at length this was too much for him, it affected his mind so strongly that his dreams were coloured by it, and the secret was partially discovered to Lady Langdale by his startling utterances when awakening from uneasy dreams. Pressed home for the truth, he was compelled to own it; although making as light of it as possible, the woman's insight saw deeper than he intended, and hence, with a gentle, but firm insistance, she gradually persuaded him to abandon their remaining journey, and at once commence retrenchment and return.

This was very hard, for they were now in sight of the mountains—the well-loved, well-remembered mountains, where Lady Langdale and her husband had passed that delicious epoch of earliest wedded love, and to whose scenes they had long yearned to go again with their children, and there recal the days of old.

Alas! to be in sight of the "promised land," and have then to return through the desert, was bitter disappointment; but to know that it was not to the old Home they were returning was bitter still. They felt like outcasts, for whom henceforth the world would have no recognised place—or like passengers adrift in a frail boat, after the wreck of a gallant ship.

Lady Langdale, of course, thought of little save how best to sustain and comfort her husband, and he needed it sorely, for in his cup of bitterness, shame and self-reproach were blended with anxiety.

" How could I be so blind a fool as to risk this ? " he would say. " You know my motive, dear ones ; it was, of course, to add to your means of innocent pleasures, both now, and when I shall be no more with you ; but for a man like myself, of fairly clear judgment and knowledge of the world, to have been hoodwinked to the consequences, is almost incredible. Can it be true ? is it not still merely a horrid dream ? "

Alas ! it was, indeed, too true.

The shock to Mildred was that of a vague, scarcely-understood sorrow ; to Gilbert it was for the moment terrible ; for, like a crash of sudden thunder, it at once revealed and destroyed his love. Yes, in that hour of sorrowful parting with Mary Grahame, which the breaking up of their plans involved, he

was first conscious of how deeply and madly
he loved her, and at the same time saw "No
Hope" written over "Love." It was as if a
fairy had risen out the ocean of life, and wandered with him for a while, making earth a
heaven, and then, just as he was about to take
her hand, receding far and farther away into
cloudland.

To Mary herself, this sudden misfortune
to her new-found friends was distressing, bewildering; but in her heart's depth of sorrow
for them, was a little faint light of almost joy;
for would not this, in years yet to come, bring
Gilbert nearer to her in station?

The same thought was underlying Caroline's sorrow—the same faint, nebulous light
of hope, made more perceptible by reason of
the present darkness. But when the first
shock of the news had been borne by all in
their several ways, there came some light

through the cloud to each. Sir Geoffrey's first regret at having recently resigned his official appointment, changed to a feeling of relief when he considered that he would else have had to do so now, and thus would have had the pain of notoriety attaching to that resignation.

He next remembered, with unmingled satisfaction, that he had caused his wife's small fortune to be settled on herself, and had made such addition to that settlement as would now, even in the worse case, secure them from absolute want. Hence, though the ship was wrecked, there was still the life-boat.

He had written at once to his brother and Sir George Blandville, and now handed his wife their characteristic answers. The latter wrote copiously, volunteering the best legal advice he could give to his friend, and although his letter was fearfully technical, and, of course, a shade pompous and patronising, still it was alike kind and useful. It contained, as an enclosure, a note from Lady Blandville, full of immense commiseration, and bristling with regrets and sorrow, etc., etc., but the velvet paw could not refrain from just a little scratch or two at the end.

William Langdale's was as hearty and thoroughly English as might have been fully expected by any one who knew what a tender heart was hidden under that rough exterior. It ran thus :—

" DEAR OLD GEOFFREY,

"Don't bother yourself about this ugly business ; the d——d rascals have certainly got the whip-hand of you, and I know it must be very mortifying and all that, especially to a proud, sensitive fellow like you; but what does it really matter? You know I've plenty of money for both of us. I've neither chick nor child to leave it to; Ann is handsomely provided for, and I really haven't any use for half what I've got, so that you're more than welcome to what ever you like. If you and your boy Gilbert would come and take some of my business cares off my shoulders, I should really be very much obliged to you, but don't trouble yourself about that either just now. You'll have a great many other matters to see to on your return. Give our love to the wife and the dear girls, and tell Gilbert to cram Charter-Party, Averages, Barter and Discounts, hard, and we'll see what we can do to make a merchant of him.

"Yours truly,

"WILLIAM LANGDALE."

This also had an enclosure, a bright, hopeful cheery note from Mrs. Langdale, with
some bits of delightfully-true womanly
sympathy thrown in most unostentatiously,
that brought happy tears to Lady Langdale's
eyes.   They were all to come, directly they
returned, to Langdale House, and stay as long
as they possibly could, and when they were
tired of London, she herself had long been
desiring a country house for the summer
months, and they could choose one altogether, or near to one another. It contained a
P.S. for Carrie, which made that young lady's
heart beat somewhat rapidly, for it told of
visits from Mr. Pierce Falconer, and what
Mr. Pierce had incoherently uttered on that
occasion, also of a later visit from Mr. Fallington, and what that gentle and still faithful
swain had also said, ending up with a little

bit of banter for Miss Carrie on the devoted faith of her two admirers.

Now all this was very cheering, but Sir Geoffrey felt he could not accept his brother's most kind and generous proposal whilst there was a possibility of independence; the stern facts that stared him in the face had to be faced. Now that there was no longer the dreadful secret, his native courage and buoyancy came back, and with it the habit of instant decision and prompt action. When they arrived in prosperous Liverpool, on their homeward track, he sold the two hunters and relay of carriage horses, and if he could have found a purchaser, would have parted with the others and the carriage also, and returned by coach, but found that involved too heavy a sacrifice.

'Twas rather with the feeling of an army

in retreat after a terrible defeat that our
poor friends retraced their way to the great
metropolis. A touch of deep-felt tender
mournfulness could hardly help making itself
visible at times to each in turn ; but each in
turn took up the character of " Cheerer
in Ordinary " to the rest, and, by pointing
out the little gleams of hope on the horizon
dispelled the gloom of the immediate present.
Thus bearing one another's burdens with as
much bravery as their several philosophies
could achieve, they arrived with a fair show
of cheerfulness once more at Richmond.
Here, however, poor Mary Grahame fairly
broke down, and on the eve of the final
parting with the friends whom she loved so
dearly for their thousand kindnesses, the
poor young girlie wept long and bitterly
by herself; and when she managed to regain
some little self-control so as to venture down

in the dusky twilight, she clung to Lady Langdale and the girls with a terrible and heart-breaking presentiment that they would never all meet again.

The return to such a dreary home as hers, was in its way, almost worse than the return of the Langdale's to no home at all; and although, of course, the poor girl tried hard to ignore the fact that there was still deeper cause for her tears, still that fact would force itself across her thoughts, despite all her efforts to disbelieve it.

In their conversations on the road and at their evening halting-places, her young and simple mind had been painfully enlightened as to the stern necessities of life and the penalties that awaited a defiance of those hard needs. Sir Geoffrey and Lady Langdale had purposely taken all the young people fully into their confidence as to the possible future, and

Mary had thus heard all their plans, and ways and means calmly and clearly discussed and explained, hence her first gleam of light as to Gilbert being brought nearer to her in station had gone dark, for Dame Fortune had now played see-saw with the two young people, and although she had wildly delightful dreams of bestowing all her little property on him, when it should come to her, she was horrified with herself for daring to look forward to that time, involving as it did the death of her father and mother. What a spider-web of bewilderment and perplexity the poor child had spun round her gentle heart. She did, and yet she did not, dare to think that Gilbert loved her. She sorrowed, and yet had a kind of gladness, in his reverses. She grieved bitterly for her dear kind friends, and longed to be her own mistress, so as to aid them, and then shrank back, cowering

with shame and self-reproach, at such a
wish.

Meantime poor Gilbert was not exactly on
a bed of roses. Whatever doubt Mary
might have about his love, he was painfully
free from any himself. The bright merry
child, the tantalizing piquante little coquette
had successively played their parts in this
little life-drama, and now touched by the
hand of sorrow. Mary Grahame stood
confest before him as a tender and noble-
hearted girl with all those deep, loving, and
earnest sympathies which stamped her (to
his eyes at least), as but a little lower than
the angels. The patronising and then petting
air with which he had first treated her had
indeed soon passed into a very different feeling, but now that feeling deepened to its
fullest intensity, and he knew that it was
love. As to whether she in any large measure

returned it, he was not coxcomb enough to
believe. He thought he was not wholly indifferent to her, and had had bright imagin-
ings of some day winning a delicious certainty;
but now, "oh, ruthless destiny, why wilt
thou dash down our wine cups, ere they be
half-filled with the forbidden nectar?"

A heavy evening this for all our friends!
Even after the most prosperous and enjoyable
journeyings, when the first of a little band
endeared to each other by many mutual
pleasures and kindnesses, breaks away from
us, and we see his or her face no more, we
feel a void, an uneasy craving for another
touch of the friendly hand, another glimpse
of the sweet smile; for alas, is it likely in the
harsh calculation of chances, that as we *have
been* we shall *ever be* again? We may cheat
our regrets by valiantly and fervently assert-
ing that we will all journey together next

year, but what a hollow, flimsy cheatery this
is—do we not know when we part, that such
parting is but the type, the forerunner of
that longer journey which we must each in
turn take alone?

Does nature sympathize with the sorrows of
us poor mortals, or was it in very truth a
lurid lowering evening? Did the black woods,
stretching away far as the eye could reach,
really put on the same dark gloom that op-
pressed their hearts; was the river like lead
for heaviness, and was the air stifling in its
hot stillness; its exhausted calm making
breathing very difficult, and sighing very
natural; and, by-and-bye did heavy drops of
rain fall with a dull muffled sound upon the
earth, as if the murky clouds had long pent
them up, and even now would fain conceal
them? And did the ever-kindly earth receive
them softly, and help to hide them, and dry

them quickly up, and give forth a fragrant and refreshing perfume of sympathy? I know not, but, oh, believe it, poor aching, sorrowing hearts; 'twill soothe ye to think that Nature mourns with you; and why should she not? Are we not her children?

It is not well to expatiate upon the inevitable glooms of life; they have to be borne by all at some time, and most of us can easily fill up such pictures with touches of personal experience—'tis more avail to remind each other how well and bravely men and women can, and do, bear up against the wrecks and racks of fortune.

Although Sir Geoffrey had received full confirmation of the complete loss of all personal possessions that this disaster would involve, he yet felt a certain buoyancy beyond mere calm endurance of the inevitable.

Happily for himself and his family, he had the temperament which inspires the leaders of " Forlorn Hopes," and the men who man the lifeboat. Danger exhilarated and calmed him. Difficulty brought with it clearness of head and decision of action. Careless, almost indolent and wavering, in the lesser crises of life, when there was really something to grapple with, he roused himself to his full strength, and delighted in that strength. Many a time, in a long career, he had crossed swords with danger, and even with death. In peril he had consciously stood on the edge of his own grave, and dared to look down into it with unflinching eyes. Not with the contemptuous indifference of the cynic or the stoic; not with the trained hardihood of the Spartan or Gladiator, but with the firm, trustful courage that comes from a higher source. Thus, whilst health and strength remained, he hoped all things, and feared nothing.

At Richmond he found a purchaser for his barouche and horses, so sending on their luggage by the carrier to Langdale House, they themselves re-entered London in a hack-carriage, the wretched horses of which were a painful contrast to their own gallant pair; but they only laughed at the sorry equipage as they passed through the splendid throng in Hyde Park, and agreed that it was better to get used as quickly as possible to their altered circumstances.

" Kings have often left their capital as we did, in a species of mild triumph," said Sir Geoffrey, "and returned, as we do, to find their kingdoms taken from them in their absence."

"What kings have had to endure, may surely be borne by us," said Lady Langdale.

"I'm glad we hadn't to ride in on these scarecrow hacks, the people would have taken us for a brace of King Richards, and thrown dust and ashes on our kingly heads."

"They are throwing quite enough dust on our bonnets already," said Mildred.

"It is a comfort we are not on the way to the Tower in the old royal fashion."

"No, it would not do for any of us to lose our heads just now, Miss Carrie."

"Or our hearts either," thought Gilbert, with a sigh.

A warm welcome awaited them at Langdale House, where they stayed for some weeks, finally arranging their future plans. William Langdale soon saw that it was no use urging his generous offer on his brother at present, since the latter had decided, for many reasons, to make a bold and independent fight to retrieve his fortunes. By the

aid of Sir George, and the skilled subordinate
legal assistance which he designated for the
purpose, all future claims upon Sir Geoffrey
were cleared by the surrender of all his
present possessions, including, of course,
Wolfern Chace, and its contents.

In a few weeks Sir Geoffrey had organised
his new career for Gilbert and himself, taken
a humble little country cottage within four
miles walk of London, and they at once settled
down to begin life anew in their altered
circumstances.

Sir Geoffrey counted now on his foregone
experiments and discoveries for yielding
back by degrees the wealth he had expended
on them, and these enterprises threw him
into frequent intercourse with Noulaiton.
Gilbert, with the infatuation of youth, believed
strongly in the possibility of turning his
poetic genius to practical account, and,

although heartily aiding Sir Geoffrey, gave
much time and thought to the completion,
and final polish, of a poem he had long been
working out. When this was ready he wrote
to Dr. Maxwell to ask an introduction to
suitable publishers, and that worthy old
gentleman rode up to town on his sturdy
sleek cob to make the introduction personally, instead of by letter.

By the kind, but unworldly Doctor, therefore, Gilbert was taken to the eminent House
of Gush, Surly, Sly and Co. (and Co. and Co.
and Co. for quite an indefinite number of
Co.'s). Gush, the head of the firm, was a portly,
almost Falstaffian personage—with a fringe
of white hair round a shining bald head, and
bushy grey whiskers of the form sometimes
irreverently characterized as "mutton-chop"
—that is, they formed an irregular triangle,
with their apexes merged in the aforesaid

fringe, and their bases (sharply defined by the
razor) resting on the edges of the volumi-
nous cravat, which, from its depth and stiffness, painfully suggested a possible apoplexy.
A rubious chin of large proportions ; smooth,
red, and angry with its morning shave,
reposed heavily on the snowy cravat, crushing it down into uneasy wrinkles.   This
cravat was a study,—the anxious care evidently bestowed upon its exact tie would
have done credit to Brummell himself ; and
its folds were so numerous and ample that,
turned to other purposes, it would have fully
provided a large baby with swaddling clothes.
Beneath this, came frothing out a snowy-drift
of shirt frills, as much as to say—" Look at
me ! See how clean I am ! " Yet the eye
rested not too long on these lower avalanches,
being attracted upward by the roseate glow
on the nose and cheeks, and by the blink of

benevolent-looking spectacles, behind which the somewhat dim lustre of a pair of treacle eyes was visible. These eyes had, what a turncock would have described, as "a little water ready laid on," which gave them a perennial dewiness, not amounting to tears, but very near it.

Besides the water, Mr. Gush had also a good deal of the milk of human kindness in him, only that it had an ugly trick of turning sour when he was angered; and, despite his overflowing benevolence, I regret to say that he was not unfrequently in a very considerable state of pepper about very trifling things—in fact, he was one of that numerous class of mortals who are exceedingly sweet-tempered when they are not vexed. But in his grand moods—in the first opening of a promising business transaction—his benignant suavity, his Quixotic super-chivalric sense of honour, his indignant denunciation and contemptuous repudiation of any but the highest and noblest modes of conducting business were blissful; almost angelic. Then it was that the mildly-brown treacle eyes gleamed and glistened over the rims of his spectacles with the aforesaid half-tear. Then it was that the oiliness and salviness of the inner man glowed and glistened over his visage with their transfiguring power, until the plump gentleman in his study chair was suggestive of nothing lower in creation than a tail-coated and black-breeched Seraph.

He was the head of the firm, and in that capacity, woe to the unlucky wight who forgot due respect to his dignity. " Let us be dignified or die," was his unuttered but enacted motto. To him, therefore, was deferentially assigned the first part in opening every important negotiation, or at least of seeming to open it. Sly, indeed, enacted jackal, but was cunning enough to let it always be supposed that the royal beast did his own catching, as well as killing.

Surly, the second partner in the firm, was a gloomy middle-aged person, who would . have been tall if Fate had not laid a heavy hand on his head, and held him down during his time of growth. His legs suggested a pair of stout lorgnettes, nearly closed up; his body a squat kettle-drum; and his head the upper-half of a cottage loaf surmounted by a black and bristly hearth-broom. He was strictly monosyllabic in conversation, and seldom condescended to give more than a curt " yes " or " no " to any enquiry; and this with various degrees of gruffness, pro-portioned to his hatred of the questioner, and the state of his own digestion.

Probably it was the habitually unsatisfactory condition of his digestion, that gave him this chronic hatred and contempt for mankind in general, and authors in particular; and that also might account for the mental atmosphere of gloom and grump in which he "lived and moved and had his being;" and which returned the compliment by "living and moving" with him wherever he went. The only way in which he could at all hold his own in business matters against his partners was by a dogged impenetrable obstinacy, which in his mind occupied the place of reason. His process of argument was deliciously simple; he merely evolved from the occult depths of his inner consciousness an assertion—a conclusion, without either major or minor premiss for its parents, and by incessant reiteration of this assertion, rapidly convinced himself of its irrefutable, absolute, pure logic. For example, just before our friends called, the firm had held a discussion on an important business question. Gush had given it as his opinion that the copy-right of "How to Cook Mushrooms in a Hundred Ways" was not worth the £1,000 that Lady Blank demanded for it.

"It's worth that if it's worth a penny," blurted out Surly.

" But, sir," returned the chief with dignity, " remember we lost money upon her former work of 'How to Bring up a Hen like a Hen on 2d. a week.'"

" It's worth that if it's worth a penny."

"But, my dear sir," says Sly, "don't you really agree with me that this kind of thing is just a leetle overdone now-a-days? and besides, if we hold back and do not seem too eager, I have information that assures me we shall get it for £900 ; possibly for much less."

"It's worth £1,000 if it's worth a penny."

"But why, Mr. Surly," returns the chief, "why, if we have a fair chance of getting the copyright for so much less, why should we give more?"

"It's worth a £1,000 if it's worth a penny."

The other two exchanged hopeless glances, accompanied by a significant shrug, but as they had reasons for not wishing to offend their *confrère*, they yielded the point. So the "mushroom" brochure got itself cooked with gold sauce, and in due time was plentifully buttered with unctuous praise in the columns of a most learned and literary weekly.

Mr. Surly having gained his point in true British style by not knowing when he was beaten, retired to his own special den with a grump and a growl that in another man might have meant satisfaction, but 'twas the nature of the man to take his pleasure not so much sadly as sulkily, as though it were a species of affront for any one to suppose that *he* could be pleased with anything. Doubtless this ungentle monster had many good qualities, but they were not strikingly apparent to strangers, hence he was generally manœuvred out of the way at first interviews. When our friends entered, therefore, they were introduced to the Head by the deferential Sly, who having first caught Dr. Maxwell, had through him caught Gilbert. Far, however, from enacting lion, Mr. Gush now, perhaps, bore a nearer resemblance to a capacious serpent gently slavering his prey before bolting it. Beaming over the edges of his glasses, he surveyed his visitors with a " Bless you, my children " air, and condescended to be as deferential as Sly himself.

" My learned friends, Dr. Maxwell and Mr.

Langdale (Is it Mr. Langdale I have the honour of addressing?) Yes, well, Doctor Maxwell and Mr. Langdale are far better judges of literature than we mere men of business; but, gentlemen, we can perhaps assist you, and permit me to say for our firm that it never, no, I may say never, promised what it was not prepared to perform!"

" Hem," thought Gilbert, " not a very terrific pledge that."

" Thank you, Mr. Gush," said Doctor Maxwell. " I was quite certain that my young friend would be in good hands in your house."

A queer twitch at the corner of Sly's mouth came and went like the windy smile of an infant when the angels are poetically supposed to be whispering to it; and Gush resumed—" You must know, Mr. Langdale, the immense difficulty of pushing poetry now-

a-days, unless it be written by a lord, a banker,
or—or an Atheist."

" Or, unless Mr. Langdale is prepared to
go into the matter boldly, and with the spirit
of a genius, who knows his own power, and
determines to let the world know it too,"
chimed in Sly.

This struck a key-note—Jackal had done
it !—Gilbert, with the impetuosity of genius,
saw nothing, cared for nothing, but that the
world should be lifted nearer Heaven by his
inspirations.

There was something in the tone of the
voice, however, that caused him to look
critically at the last speaker to see whether
this was the true ring or the counterfeit
Mr. Sly's eyes did not exactly meet the look,
but the gentleman himself was, in appearance, by no means the " foxy Modred " that
his name seemed to suggest.   A small dapper

figure, and almost girlish in feature, with a
light pinky complexion, downy, dawning
whiskers and fair hair. To a casual
observer he seemed (if it were necessary
to classify him at all) to belong to the un-
feathered " pigeon " tribe rather than to the
" rooks ;" but then this was only a part of
his slyness, in which Nature had maliciously
assisted him. In reality, he did the utmost
honour to his name, and deserved it
splendidly. He was a man who, if there were
a roundabout way and a straight way of doing
a thing, would strenuously and cunningly
take the roundabout; and this circumambient
sagacity was immensely admired by his
senior. For how much more clever the cat
appears who walks round the mouse instead
of vulgarly pouncing upon it at a single
leap. Unfortunately, slyness being not
always wisdom, but only a plausible imitation

of it, the financial interests of the house had occasionally suffered heavily from Mr. Sly's double-cunning. Surly was a little apt to growl at this, but Sly having cleverly taken the measure of Mr. Gush's foot, knew when and where to kiss it meekly, and never trod on his corns like Surly. So the two first were more than a match for the last, who could not often do more than growl to himself in his den, or vent his wrath upon meek clerks and terrified printers' devils. To this pleasant gentleman, however, Gilbert was introduced by Gush in passing out, because, as the latter sagely observed, " Mr. Langdale will have, occasionally, to transact business with all the members of the firm."

Then turning to Doctor Maxwell, he further explained, " You see, Doctor Maxwell, order is the soul of business—and we each have our departments with which the others

do not interfere.   I bring my long experience
to bear upon the acceptance or rejection of
the literary productions offered to us.   Mr.
Sly carries out the arrangements of the
'issue,' and Mr. Surly is accountable to our
clients for the returns."

A more judicious appointment of parts
could hardly have been conceived, for Mr.
Surly was the *beau ideal* of a man to over-
awe and snub an unlucky author who might
be a little impatient for his returns.

When the two friends emerged from the
palatial offices of this omnipotent triumvirate,
Doctor Maxwell was scared to hear the
arrangement Gilbert had been led into by
Sly, whilst Gush had held him in lofty and
philanthropic conversation.

"Sixty guineas for the publication, and
two hundred for announcements to begin
with.   You to take all risk, and they to have

a ten per cent. on advertisments, and a ten per cent. on sales! Why, Gilbert, what could you have been thinking of?"

"Well, sir, to say the truth, I was not thinking about the money at all; but Mr. Sly assures me that their house paid * * * four thousand pounds for his half-year's work; and if once my name gets fairly before the public, there is no reason why I should not draw upon them for some such figure."

"Ah, but he did not tell you that * * *'s first issue of five hundred copies took ten years to sell (and give away) during which time he was, perhaps, the best abused man in the three kingdoms, especially in the northern third."

"Troy after ten years," mused Gilbert, half-aloud. "But still, Troy was taken—a long time—a weary siege—but still, Troy was taken. Yes," he exclaimed, with rising enthu-

siasm, "I can wait—I can fight—despite of
the 'Scots, wha' hae!'"

"Oh, you can wait, and you can fight—no
doubt," said the Doctor, "but what are you
to do for the sinews of war, my young
friend? Mr. Gush most sagely remarked,
that only a lord or a banker could expect any
sudden popularity; and they get it by a parody
of the Scriptural text of 'to him who hath,
shall be given."

"Ah well, I must appeal to another text
for my consolation—'sufficient unto the day
is the evil thereof.' I've got a five hundred
left of my grandfather's legacy, and when
that's gone, or before, perhaps, I must do
hackwork, and make my worse pay for my
better labours—but come, here we are at
Temple Bar; let's take a chop and a modest
pint of port at the Cock, and have 'a good
talk,' as old Dr. Johnson used to say."

The, friends did as Gilbert suggested, and the conversation gradually drifted away from the pounds, shillings, and pence of literature to the object, motive, and power of poetry as one of its forms. Of course Gilbert took the high view, that the form and manner metrical was but as the body to the soul, and that the highest skill and ingenuity in the measurement of syllables, the construction of cadences, and the positioning of rhymes does not constitute a poet in any thing like the high sense.

" But tell me, Doctor," he resumed, " why is it that poetry is rapidly losing its hold on the public mind ? "

" Well, sir, there are three reasons. Firstly, we are a practical, money-loving, money-needing people, and poetry does not pay; secondly, because the critics find it gives them more trouble to review than prose; also that they sometimes make egregious mistakes in their estimate of some new writers; hence they have determined to discourage all, and scoff at them with every possible expression of contempt that they can lay their pens upon; in point of fact, and avowedly, to " put Poetry down"—and thirdly, because the Lord, the Banker, and the Atheist aforesaid, being the three sole recognised exponents of the Poetry of the Age, people read their productions, not because they like them, but because everybody talks about them. Very well; the average common-sense Briton is not by any means a fool—and when he finds in the lordling's effusions a sham misanthropy uttered in grandly-rounded, sonorous stanzas, and ' voices full of sound and fury signifying nothing,' he is apt to get confused, and a shade dizzy, with the mellifluous morbidities. He turns for relief and quiet to the banker's

Italian cream—but this, though eminently soothing, is provocative of drowsiness, and not unfrequently is suggestive of milk and water. So then he makes a bold dash into the latest ravings of Atheistic poetry, and finds there ample cause to open his eyes, indeed, and to awaken him up thoroughly; but happily, it awakens at the same time a strong and honest disgust at the ostentatious impieties and sensualisms of genius gone—mad."

" But whilst such poetry as Wordsworth's, Southey's, Coleridge's and many other true and noble leaders of thought is given to the world, why does the world doff it aside ?"

" Because, dear boy, from the very fact of its being high, it must of necessity be above the common level. The leaders—or, as you might more truly call them—pioneers of thought, must march in advance of their age.

Like the great leader, who delivered the Israelites from Egypt, they must pass up into the cloudy heights of their Sinai and be lost to sight, and almost to recollection, for a time. Meanwhile, the people make to themselves a golden calf—a glorified exemplar of their own calfishness. This they place upon a pedestal, not greatly elevated above their own standpoint, and fall down and freely worship themselves in it."

"Your metaphor might be strained yet further, if in the grand poet of each age, we recognise the modern type of the ancient prophet bringing down clearly-written commandments on tablets of enduring stone."

"Yes, and the world does recognise that; but not till the prophet is grey with age, and weary and worn with long wrestling. But, to change the metaphor, let us accept the idea of the poet as a teacher of finely subtle

truth; such truth being manifest to him by
the intuition of genius, but obviously not
manifest to the average mind;—else all men
would be poets. The world, therefore, has
to be educated up to his standpoint before it
can see with his eyes or appreciate his subtlety.
Now this process (in which you must remember he is a chief agent) is a long one, requir-
ing sometimes ten, sometimes twenty, sometimes thirty years—during all which time the
average men and women of his age naturally
and inevitably look upon him as either a fool,
a dreamer, or a madman, according to their
several tastes in epithets."

" Of course, and the higher the wisdom the
more foolish it seems to the fool."

" Most certainly; and it is curious to see
how nearly every generation repeats pre-
cisely the same career, the worship of the
golden calf in its youth, and a returning

reverence for the tablets of stone in its matu-
rity. Sometimes, unfortunately for the
bringer-down of the higher law, the tablets
of stone are only used for his tombstone."

"Accept the inevitable! It is useless to
cavil at the 'What is, the what has been, and
what ever will be in this life.' Still, if you
prefer it, it is not impossible that you might
be a golden calf."

"Thank you; but what if I proved to be
the calf without its glittering adjective?"

"Oh, that also is possible, very possible."

"I'll not risk it—if a man acts up to his
highest convictions—obeys the noblest motives of which he is conscious, and still fails to
leave a mark upon his age, it is a failure that
carries no shame with it; but if he sets aside
these motives for the vulgar vanity of winning
quick and noisy applause, a mushroom fame
and a larger share of the gilt-gingerbread of

life, success would be more or less poisoned by inner self-contempt, and failure would sink him in the deepest and most abject self-abasement."

"Probably there could be few mental tortures keener than for a man to have to confess at his life's end—' I sacrificed what I knew to be a noble impulse at such and such a time in order to flatter the reigning folly of the hour; and the reigning folly scorned my flattery. I neglected a high task that was placed for me to do, in order that I might cleverly spice the cup of debauchery, or make the 'groundlings' laugh and applaud; and my clever spice was thrown back at me with disgust, and my Tomfool antics were hissed.' "

" Not agreeable, certainly ; but unluckily a great many (myself included, I fear) must cut some Tomfool antics to keep the wolf from the door ; like poor Grimaldi, we must grin to live."

" Not so. Because a man has literary power which he feels can be turned to good use, is he compelled therefore to devote himself wholly and exclusively to literary work ? Better a thousand times to take up some other career (however prosaic) whereby to win his daily bread, than use his pen to prick his conscience."

" But does not a life of drudgery and business destroy the fineness of the intellectual vision ? "

" It may destroy its *finesse;* its feverish super-sensitiveness ; but what it loses in that direction is compensated by a greater vigour in another. Shakspeare would not have been so perfect a dramatist if he had not been also a strong-willed, clear-headed man of business, and 'Paradise Lost' was not spoilt by foreign despatches."

" You believe then that genius is irrepressible, and must display its light even in the darkest circumstances ? "

" Does not the whole history of literature show this ? But even if it were not so, better that its light should be extinguished, or used in the humblest vocation, than perverted to throw a false glitter on vice, or to lead the unwary astray. When the beacon of warning and guidance is used as a Will-o'-the-wisp, it is a deadly curse to the age; for where genius leads, a hundred lesser lights follow, and thousands are thus enticed into the sickly unwholesome swamp."

" There is no doubt that literary powers are a heavy responsibility."

" Yes, and yet nothing is made so light of.

A clever man throws up a feather to see which way the popular wind blows, and then trims his sails to catch it with the utmost self-satisfaction and complacency."

"And with the most sublime indifference as to where it carries him and his passengers, so long as they pay him handsomely for the passage."

"Ah! pay, pay; the sternest master in the whole world is the paymaster. But now, dear boy, we also must first pay for, and then leave, our port."

"Can we be said to leave what has already gone?" retorted Gilbert, as arm in arm they sallied out into the stream of human life.

At this hour that ceaseless stream was setting steadily west, towards Drury Lane, Covent Garden, and the little theatre in the Haymarket. The bankers and wealthy merchants, with their wives and daughters in the old family carriage, driven by the portly magnificent coachman, enthroned on a still more magnificent hammer-cloth, with one or two footmen standing behind. The well-to-do tradesman and his family in the never-to-be-forgotten " Hackney Coach," a wondrous vehicle with the insignia of past grandeur still visible on its cracked and weather-worn panels. These old affairs were never built for their specific purpose, but were the semi-decayed carriages of the nobility and merchants of a former decade. An air of faded magnificence invested them with a melancholy interest, and one could moralize upon the mutability of human grandeur in a Hackney coach in a very satisfactory manner. Quite another train of thought, however, was suggested by the unusual luxury of a ride in a coach, to the little misses and masters Smith, Brown, or Jones, who in their passage past the lamp-lighted shops, *en route* for the pantomime, flattened their poor little noses distressingly against the rattling plate-glass windows, in their intense eagerness to see everything that was to be seen in London streets.

On the footways was a less rapid but more continuous stream. Country folk in leathern gaiters, fluffy beaver hats and miraculous waistcoats ; flabby pale-faced shopkeepers, in greasy black suits, dingy shirts, and dubiously white cravats, loudly dressed clerks of the Dick Swiveller order, and a great many imitations of gentlemen, none of them wholly satisfactory or successful, were interspersed with the sempiternal "rough," and the ever ubiquitous London boy. The London boys of that age were worth notice, for they had a vast deal of natural humour. It used to be a point of honour with them to have some stock saying, which was often applied very wittily. For example, when that monstrous feminine head gear was in fashion, composed of concentric circles of bows and ribbons coiled round a straw hat, with a brim as broad as a young umbrella, it was quite in accordance with the fitness of things that the wearers should be greeted with the remark of—" All round your 'at," and when a nervous old gentleman was pausing on the edge of a crossing, " Does your mother know you're out?" was at once a pertinent and an impertinent enquiry; whilst to an inebriated late reveller vainly endeavouring to stop his keyhole from going round—the assurance "that you don't lodge here, Mr. Ferguson," was appropriate, even if rude.

Slowly making headway against this tide of motley life, our two friends passed on to the quiet, nearly deserted streets of the central City, and thence to the unsavoury eastern thoroughfare yclept Shoreditch. Here the London boy was wholly merged in the youthful "Rough" in its roughest form. Fearfully repulsive women, half unsexed by coarse debauchery and shrewish passions— men with cut-throat, hang-dog visages and savage, furtive eyes; squalid, ragged children swarmed, and seethed, and wriggled in a thick, grimy atmosphere, laden with vile smells from tainted meat, fried fish, and train oil lamps; which last cast a smoky, lurid glare upon the whole scene, making it inexpressibly hideous.

Such were the sights and odours that smote upon their eyes and disgusted their nostrils; whilst their ears were assailed with every possible discord of cry, yell, and oath that it could ever enter into the mind of man to conceive, or his mouth to utter. A far worse Pandemonium this seemed to Gilbert than the wild picture he had recently witnessed in the Black Country, because here crime and vice lurked under the inevitable unsightliness of the lowest types of human form.

The horrors of this middle passage depressed both the travellers to a wondering, saddened silence, and it was not till they had escaped through a dingy lane leading out of the Hackney Road into the then desolate and dangerous open space called the "London Fields," that either of them broke silence or even drew a free breath. There they paused, as by a common instinct, and turned to look back on the dull red glare they had just left behind them.

The cries, yells and oaths that were still being hurled up into the heavens, were now

merged in one sullen, hoarse roar, mingling
with the louder roar of traffic on its ten
thousand wheels; but Dr. Maxwell, turning
to Gilbert, said—

"Cannot one understand from this wretched
scene through which we have passed something of the feeling with which Lot escaped
from the doomed cities of the plains?"

"I can, vividly," replied Gilbert. "I remember the first time I passed through those
horrid purlieus alone, late one Saturday
night; I turned to look back, fully expecting
to see the flames burst forth, or the fire de-
scend from the outraged Heavens."

"'Tis a wonder that the awful smoulder-
ing passions lurking in every street, court,
and alley do not absolutely, and from mere
natural causes, burst forth into a general
conflagration. Drunken idiocy, mad rage,
reckless wickedness, each and all trusted with

fire in all its shapes, uncontrolled and un-
guarded, through the long secret hours of the
winter's nights."

" One need not, indeed, imagine the fiery
hail from above; all the elements of fiercest
destruction are already there, and seem merely
held in check for a time by a miracle of
merciful Providence."

" Aye, long suffering, and desiring not the
death of sinners, ' but rather that they should
turn from their wickedness and live.' "

" Upon no other hypothesis is it possible to
account for the nightly marvel of an uncon-
sumed city. Say that only half a score out
of half a million of those reckless heathens
were to fire, by thievish design or drunken
accident, ten of those tumbledown, wide-
lying homes on one night, what could our
penny squirts of parish engines do to cope
with such a bewildering event? "

"Or what avail would be the poor old women, satirically called 'Watchmen,' to control the savagery of the excited mob?"

"'Twould be a perilous night for London."

"Yes, for fire involves robbery and murder as well as smoke."

"Nothing, perhaps, makes a mob more ferociously savage and uncontrollable; 'tis something akin to the red fever which young soldiers experience in their first battles; the roar of flame, the crackling detonations of the bursting timbers, the crashing down of walls, rouse a kind of flame-delirium and a wild craving for more fire, more crashing, more destruction."

"'Tis this frenzy that causes some of the wilder maniacs to cut the hose pipes, and thus side with the destroyer, I suppose."

"Very probably, unless when private malice is the prompter."

Our friends had thus drifted down in thought from the doomed cities of the plain to modern hose-pipes, and, meantime, had prosaically plodded their way half across the diagonal field foothpath that led from the classic region of the Hackney Road to the once Cockney Paradise called Hackney.

These London Fields and the adjacent Cambridge Heath, were often, in those days, the resort of a low, mean class of footpads; half-sneaking, half-savage ruffians who, like wolves, would attack the weak and defenceless when they themselves were in strong muster, but would merely snarl and run away if they were boldly met. These delightful members of society bore about the same relation to the aristocratic highwayman of Hounslow as they themselves bore to the mere pickpocket; they were a kind of middle class between Claude Duval and the Artful

Dodger, combining in themselves the very
worst qualities of each.

By the time the travellers had reached the
middle of the Fields a clammy mist had come
crawling towards town from the sluggish Lea
and the dank Essex marshes. Although it
had not yet attained to the dignity of a real
London fog, it yet made every object very ob-
scure.

In this *chiaroscuro* was dimly visible the
figure of what seemed a supernaturally tall
man stalking on slowly before them and talking loudly to himself. Two voices were distinctly audible as they gradually gained upon
him, and yet no other figure came into view
with whom he could conceivably have been
conversing.

This was, as our Northern friends say,
"uncanny," and the only solutions of the
mystery that suggested themselves were that

the person whom they were gradually approaching was a large lunatic let out during a lucid interval, or a giant ventriloquist from Richardson's show.

Curiosity to solve the matter made them quicken their pace until, upon nearer approach, their mysterious apparition gradually resolved itself simply into an ordinary man with a child on his shoulders, who civilly bade them good night as they passed.

Whilst they were laughing at each other's stupidity for not recognizing this possibility, a far more disagreeable incident occurred. A sound as of many feet running towards them, and the next moment five or six ill-favoured roughs drove against them with evident " malice aforethought." Gilbert reeled under the shock, but happily recovering his balance, lost no time in laying about him with his stout oak stick, taking, however, two or

three cracks on the head in the *mêlee* that
made the sparks flash in his eyes. The poor
old doctor was not so fortunate, the rascals
had aimed at him with more success; one
knocked the hat over his eyes, another butted
at him like a goat or a negro, and as the
portly gentleman bent forward with the pain,
a third dexterously abstracted the watch from
his fob and the purse from his pocket. The
whole gang then surrounded Gilbert, and it
would have fared hard with him also, but
happily their quondam giant hearing cries,
ran manfully up, shouting gruffly with his
one voice and squeaking hard in a high key
with the other, whereupon the cowardly
scoundrels took to their heels, and quickly
disappeared into their congenial mist.

John Blake, the valuable ally, who had
thus so gallantly come to the rescue, willingly
accompanied them as far as the " Old

Mermaid," in Hackney, and there as willingly accepted a glass of brandy and water, in acknowledgment of his timely succour, and strongly recommended a similar restorative to the Doctor. A fine sturdy bluff fellow was this John Blake when seen by the light of the parlour candles of the Old Mermaid; with the clear, fearless and frank independence of manner that comes from a consciousness of simple honesty and integrity of purpose. A twinkle of irrepressible fun passed over his face as he looked upon poor Dr. Maxwell's smashed hat, woe-begone countenance and deranged and dilapidated appearance; for when a very *point-device* old gentleman has been unexpectedly rumpled and crushed by any sudden disaster of this kind, the incongruity presented by the past precision of apparel and its present condition is decidedly droll. One does not notice a

rent in a home-spun garment, but if the coat
and trousers are of the glossiest and most
satiny black, and the rent reveals a very
snowy under-garment, it attracts an unpleasantly large share of attention.   Blake
was the village smith, of the quiet, out-of-
the-world hamlet, called Homerton, which lay
off about a mile beyond the square tower of
Old Hackney Church, and it was in the most
secluded part of this quiet hamlet that Sir
Geoffrey had found a little cottage suited to
his changed circumstances. The honest smith
ultimately found no reason to regret this
chance-encounter, but now they bade him
good-night, and without further adventure
found themselves very welcome in Ivy Cottage.
A plain, simple, but nicely served supper
awaited them, for supper was now the grand
meal of the day and the only one at which all
met.

Over a small bowl of whiskey-punch our two heroes fought their battles once again, to the commiseration of the ladies, and the amusement of Sir Geoffrey. Of course he was grieved and annoyed that the Doctor should have lost his watch and purse, but he knew the old gentleman was rich enough to render such a loss wholly unimportant, and, however grieved we may be, there is something in the misfortunes of our best friends not wholly tearful to us. Indeed, with some ill-regulated natures, where the sense of the ludicrous is strong, they cannot even see a friend slip down into a duck-weedy ditch, or trip and tumble forward into a nicely positioned mud-heap, without indulging in a rude peal of laughter. They are sorry for him, but being moved either to laugh or cry, they naturally prefer the former.

A chat round the fire about old times and

new plans and a good sound sleep, restored
the Doctor to perfect equanimity, and the
next morning, after Sir Geoffrey and Gilbert
had trudged off to town, the ladies amused
him by showing him over their droll little
cottage and its tiny triangular garden.
Happily this little garden opened upon
a fine broad grass field, on one side of which
the woods and plantations of the Priory appeared, only separated by a hedge and ditch
from the Langdale's garden. At the front
of the cottage, just across the roadway, corn
fields, alternated with meadow land far away
down to the banks of the Lea, and from
thence the eye took in the distant ranges of
forest land, stretching away through Walthamstow, Leytonstone, and Woodford.
With these surroundings they had still the
songs of birds, and the perfume of flowers,
the shade of trees, the freshness of the

newly mown grass, and the waving of the corn in the wind. Much happiness of a plain and simple kind was thus still within them, and with grateful hearts they put forth their hands to reach it, and made the most of it.

CHAPTER II.

WHEN Pierce Falconer left the Chace, after his dreaded interview with Sir Geoffrey, the clouds seemed to gather above and around him with an oppression that was simply crushing. The morning had been fitfully lurid, with occasional bursts of sunshine, alternating with a roaring, tearing wind that shook the leaves down in wild showers, and sent up columns of dust to dance with them in a mad Walpurgis reel in the air. In his downward ride he had been first fevered with the glare, and then chilled with the gloom and wind, but now a dull, impenetrable leaden sky seemed drooping lower and lower, and darkening deeper and deeper, until he felt like the poor wretch in the contracting torture-chamber.

Through the forest track the mis-shapen, big-headed pollards, pointed their skinny fingers at him in derision, and to his diseased imagination seemed to run after him as he sped along, whilst the great, scornful taller trees only deigned to send after him a hissing shower of their leaves. The cottage dogs hunted him, yelping out their mingled spite and contempt, and the few village children, staring up at him from their play in the ditches and from their dirt-pies in the gardens, grinned at his discomfiture, whilst the woodmen, pausing on their axes to sneer at him as he galloped past, broke into coarse jeers and brutal laughter, which he knew was excited by his haggard, wretched expression.

When, emerging from the forest track he gained the high road, it suggested to him the Scriptural sentence of—"Fast bound in misery and iron," for it echoed back the iron blows of his steed's hoofs with a hard "clang-clang" that seemed to hit him on the head like incessant hammers. The broad, bleak stretch of plain through which the slow sedgy Lea wound its serpentlike course seemed inexpressibly "flat, stale, and un-profitable," and the low line of dark back-ground beyond, frowned blackly upon him. Poor fellow, the sun was, indeed, out of his heaven, and earth was hideous! He had started at full gallop, wounded, hunted, haunted and riding madly, as if for life, to escape the impending clouds ; but on gaining the road a throbbing headache compelled him to draw rein, and to go softly on his night-mare journey. Once only he awoke to a grim saturnine smile when a small street arab shrilled out to his companion, as Falconer passed them—"Oh! cri, Bill, look there! There's a ghost a horseback!" "Alas, poor ghost," thought Pierce, "I am indeed a ghost of my former self—or worse—the living body without its soul."

Leaving the mare at the stables, he wandered restlessly and ghostlike through the crowded streets, and to and fro across the bridge; often standing back to watch the tide of life as it ebbed westward, and still more often and more dangerously watching the tide of waters as they ebbed eastward. He felt to the full that terrible fascination which a clear cool flowing river has for the fevered brain, the writhing pulse, and raging thirst of despair, and, but for the gracious sustainment which is so often granted us in our hours of darkness and

temptation Pierce Falconer would have
passed from this world on that night to a
fearful awakening.   Happily the first danger
is generally also the last; if we have but resolution to fight the demon of temptation
à outrance and at once.   Perchance angels
do come and minister to us in our deepest
despondencies; or perhaps it is well that we
should fight this fight alone.   There is more
of danger; but the victory is also more complete.

It was with a fair assumption of calmness
that Pierce met me on the following morning, and confessed that—"All was over."
There was just a tremor on the lip, and a
flush on the brow; a passing expression of
intense sorrow in the eyes, and then? Why
then Pierce Falconer bore his anguish like a
man and a Spartan, and it was at once tacitly
understood between us that the subject was

tabooed till he should choose to renew it. So we beat about the bush, with as little restraint as was possible under the circumstances, to start fresh thoughts by which this one absorbing grief might be temporarily ignored.

Now, by good hap, it chanced that there was something worth talking and thinking about; for Noulaiton, taking up the thread of investigation which Pierce had left in his hands on the day of his visit to the Chace, had suddenly found the clue to a grand discovery, which a few more weeks of patient working out, would, in all probability, perfect.

Here, then, was a potent counterspell to love, and Pierce gratefully accepted it; plunging headlong into the pursuit and making up for his lost enthusiasm by dogged resolution.

I was often with him during this trying
time of his young life, and could not but
admire the quiet courage with which he bore
his sorrow, and the self-control with which he
concealed it. It was well he did so, for the
Doctor was a born sceptic as to the power and
depth of love, which, in his vocabulary,
only meant a refined kind of intrigue, and he
would only have bantered poor Pierce to the
verge of lunacy.

Banter is a fine antidote to a superficial
passion, but to a deep, earnest, soul-absorbing
one, it is a cruel and useless insult; none the
less painful, because kindly intended.

One afternoon as Pierce and I were
together in his laboratory, we heard the
hearty laughing voice of Noulaiton preced-
ing him up the stairs; a pleasant sound, soon
followed by his own pleasanter presence.

Shaking us both in turn with both hands, and saluting Pierce, French fashion, to which the latter submitted with as much grace as is ever possible to an Englishman, he broke out into a full joyous laugh, in the intervals of which came out the following words—

"*Allons mes braves.* Victory, victory. Your grand *messieurs* of the Treasury have condescended at last to announce their august intention of not preventing us from doing the nation a great service; if—mark you well—if we succeed!"

" Magnificent," said Pierce ; " what a grand concession."

" Confound their insolence," I exclaimed.

" And their sublime apathy," added Pierce.

" Patience boys ? What will you ? We are on earth, and men are unjust to us. How puerile the complaint ; but, come, let us

make the best of it; to be permitted to do
our best is something. Let us do it, and
then grumble."

"Ah, Doctor, you have hit hard upon the
Englishman's privilege."

"Yes, his sole one, I believe."

"Bar *habeas corpus* and the charming
fiction of every Englishman's house being his
castle."

"A fiction ruthlessly destroyed by the
unpleasingly punctual invasion of the tax
collector."

"Ah, well! grumbling is a fine safety
valve; if we had suffered our *sans culottes*
to growl a little more, perhaps they would
not have bitten quite so hard when they
broke lose."

"Especially if the poor wretches had had
something else to bite at."

"Bah! I must own that we gave them

little else than bones of contention—but
enough of this; the awful wolfish howls of
that dreadful time still ring in my ears, and
a curiously unpleasant sensation about the
back of the neck attacks me when I recall
the narrow escape I had from Monsr.
Guillotin's amiable invention."

" I can well believe it ; but do not we also
lay our heads on the block for blockheads to
cut off ?"

" Rather a far-fetched simile that. I'm
afraid you had lost your head before you
made it."

" Young men always lose their heads when
they lose their temper, and Mr. Pierce Falconer is very angry with the Treasury Com-
missioners just now."

" Perhaps they will survive his wrath.
Public bodies are provokingly impersonal,
and not presenting any salient point to be

kicked, and not possessing anything but a species of corporate conscience—so divided as to be altogether invisible—they are wholly impregnable both in body and soul."

"Wholly and entirely; you could not insert a new idea into their heads even by trepanning them."

"And if you could, the idea would affect each one so differently that they would have to debate about it for a decade, and, finally, compromise both it and themselves by a colourless muddle, wherein the original intention was barely visible."

"That is to say, in coroner's language, 'Found Drowned.'"

"Exactly so. History for ever repeats itself; and not a session passes without its massacre of the Innocents."

"The part of Herod being enacted by the Prime Minister."

" Yes, and *he* is considered the primest of ministers, whose massacre is the earliest and most complete."

" So as not to interfere with the *feux de joie* in honour of St. Grouse; well we must own, however deficient the aims of our legislators in Parliament, they go straight to the mark on the moors."

" The more's the pity; they should keep their powder dry for larger game."

" Meaning deer ? "

" No; although deer-stalking in the good old-fashioned way is not bad training for the real legitimate object of the hunting instinct, still it is only 'training'; but now, the so-called "sport" is emasculated by sticking some lazy Lord Tom Noddy in a snug corner, with lots of "guides, philosophers and friends" to assist him in the use of his eye glass, and with a perfect battery of rifles; and then driving a herd of timid, stupid brutes to look down the muzzles of his guns, whilst he fires at them. Yes, and then, after many glasses of choice Madeira, my Lord Tom Noddy rides triumphantly home, and is looked upon as a mild species of hero, instead of what he really is, an amateur butcher."

"'What shall he have who killed the deer'?"

"Oh, 'his leathern coat and horns to wear,' by all means; and I think it should be incumbent on all such valorous deer-slayers to wear the coat and horns at all future Court presentations."

"The effect would be decidedly quaint and picturesque."

"Almost as much so as the Prince Regent's kilt in Edinburgh."

"Ah, 'twas the Prince himself that was

'kilt, then, entirely,' instead of the deer (as O'Sullivan would say)."

" And yet the ladies all vowed that he was ' such a dear.' "

" And they were right; there never was a Prince so dear to the nation as His Royal Highness."

Our chat had thus drifted away, as usual, into mild and merry badinage, and was only stopped by the arrival of a letter to Dr. Noulaiton from Lady Langdale, in which she told, in a few simple and touching words, the history of their sudden reverse of fortune; filling in the history with many little incidents hitherto unknown. How, for example, Sir Geoffery had ridden to the Chace on the night of their return and cut her portrait from its frame, before it could be desecrated by the rough hands of those modern harpies, who live by, and gloat over, the ruin of homes; and how poor Joe had brought over for the girls the two rose trees they had planted, and a great basket-full of fruit and eggs and butter, and could scarcely be prevailed upon to accept anything for his trouble. These and other demonstrations of kindness from their former neighbours and dependants had freshened the dear lady's heart with a feeling of much happiness. In her note she did not go through the stereotyped and unkind form of " wondering if any one would care to acknowledge them in their altered circumstances," but simply ended her letter with a " Come and see us, dear Doctor, very soon."

No second invitation was needed, you may be sure, and Pierce looked so wistfully and enquiringly at me, that I at once proposed we should all three go down together the next morning.

There was then only an old-fashioned lumbering two-horse coach that started about three times a day from the " Flower Pot" in Bishopsgate Street, and toddled slowly down, drawn by a venerable pair of horses, who had seen better days, and driven by a red-faced, plethoric, choleric old Jehu, nearly as wheezy as his horses, and very considerably fatter. So, having escorted the merry Doctor to the coach, and assisted him up to the box-seat, where he immediately extorted a hearty laugh from old " Lobster," we mounted our horses, and rode down, taking a detour and a gallop over the marshes, so as to time our arrival at the Cottage simultaneously with that of Dr. Noulaiton; because the invitation having been sent to him only, we felt as shy as school boys at the idea of going there without him.

Pierce, confided to me as we rode along

that he felt himself to be one of the most contemptible wretches in existence, because, for the life of him, he could not help rejoicing, with an exultation of which he was heartily ashamed, to think that now Caroline was at least within his reach, and that he might possibly be able to win for her a position better than her own.

" I know that I'm a selfish beast," he said. " I ought to have no feeling but that of sorrow for her reverse of fortune, but what is a poor devil to do ? he can't command or control the innermost and deepest feelings of his heart."

" No, we are but big babies still ; we look out of our windows and cry for some lovely moon, and we would prefer to pull it out of heaven, and find it nothing but a cream cheese, rather than not have our longings gratified."

" Compare me to a baby, or a booby, or a baboon, or anything else you think proper, but oblige me by not comparing Caroline Langdale to a cream cheese."

" *Crême de la crême,* dear boy ! do not take my metaphors too literally, and do not frown so Byronically; but here we are at the Cottage, and old Lobster has providentially got his stable-boy in the dickey, so we can leave our horses in his charge."

We entered all three together into the little Cottage, and were received by the ladies with infinite grace. They parried our expressions of condolence, by making great fun of their doll's-cottage, and we then sauntered through into the garden, and sat under the shadow of the one great tree, swiftly forgetting both where we were, and how long a visit we were paying, until the little maid-servant came through to say that the stable-boy in charge of our horses was obliged to go away to attend to the coach. Thereupon Lady Langdale suggested that we should have them put up at the coach yard, and stay the afternoon and evening, so as to see Sir Geoffrey and Gilbert when they came home. That arch imposter, Pierce, made a desperate show of determination to resist this delightful proposal, and if Dr. Noulaiton and I had not been perfect angels in broad-cloth, we would have punished him by taking him at his word ; but it would have been too cruel ; for never, perhaps, in this world did any two young people enjoy an afternoon as they did. After a frugal lunch, chiefly of fruits and salad, we sauntered through the lanes down to the river, and taking boat, lazily explored its little creeks and islets, and rested under the shadows of the willows ; then, as evening brought coolness, we wrapt the ladies in their shawls, called Dr. Noulaiton's attention to his duties as steersman, and enjoyed a good breathing-pull from the bridge to the first up-river lock and back again.

Soon after our return to the Cottage, Sir Geoffrey and Gilbert arrived home, and we had a charming nondescript meal, known in the north country as " High Tea," during which we managed to extract as much gaiety out of very small sources, as could be reasonably expected. Gaiety was not perhaps the word for Pierce and Caroline, for whom a higher, subtler joy was present, mostly expressed by the eyes, or with low-toned speech, forming an occasional diapason of mellowed happiness, amidst the higher notes of our lighter music.

Theirs was the almost perfect happiness of two fine natures exquisitely attuned to one another, long-parted and now once more in unison, with renewed hope, as the key-note of their melody. The *réunion* of the elders of the little party was also one of great pleasantness, and Sir Geoffrey's eyes glistened as he shook us one after another by the hand, for he felt that though stricken down in the battle of life, he had a few faithful comrades left, ready as ever to draw swords on his side.

Hence for a time that ever constant feeling of self-reproach was banished and forgotten, and we talked hopefully of the possibilities which the future had in store for all, or at least for some of us. Sir Geoffery related how he had resumed, with the stern earnestness of pressing needs, the study of the great problem which had been merely his secondary task at the Chace, and how useful an assistant he had found in Blake, whose humble shoeing-forge and four-acre field, was slowly and

cautiously undergoing a process of ex-
pansion by the addition of here a shed, and
there a lathe, and anon a rolling mill, hoisting-
gear, drills, punches and all the primitive
powers of lever, wedge and screw.

" Ha! ha! ha!" laughed Dr. Noulaiton.
You call *me* Mephistopheles, and Pierce, Dr.
Faustus; but you, my dear Sir Geoffrey, are
an absolute Tubal-cain, and your black Black-
smith a veritable modern Vulcan."

" Was not Vulcan merely a modern
Tubal-cain in his time?" asked Gilbert.

"Oh, very probably," retorted Dr. Noulaiton,
but one should never know too much of such
matters. Without a good deal of ignorance,
one could never have the bliss of a *jeu-de-
mot;* and it would sadly circumscribe the
pleasant power of calling each other bad
names if we were too accurately acquainted
with the original owners. *E non vero e bon*

trovato is a motto absolutely essential to the case of conversation."

" Why, yes," said Pierce. " Only conceive the frightful responsibility that one would feel in uttering any light thought that chances to float up to the lips if we were called upon to prove its logical and historical accuracy."

" I, for one, should never utter anything," said Mildred."

" The loss to yourself would be great, but to society simply irreparable," said Gilbert, with mock solemnity.

" If by society you mean yourself, Mr. Pert, you spoke truth without intending it. It would indeed be disastrous for you, if you were not perennially refreshed with my wisdom and wit."

" Permit me to say," chimed in Pierce, " that you, also, have spoken truth without knowing it; your unconscious wisdom and spontaneous wit refresh us all."

" Are you practising your pretty speeches on me, in order to perfect them for some one else, Mr. Falconer?"

Pierce betrayed himself instantly by a rapid glance at Caroline, and Gilbert said—

" If wisdom is unconscious, is it wisdom in the utterer? I do not wish to detract from your infinite sagacities, my dear Mildred-Minerva, but when the Delphian Priestess speaks merely as the medium of the Oracle, we accept the Oracle, but we do not compliment the Priestess."

" The poet has been studying diligently the modern guide to Olympus, ' Lempriere,' and now means to suffocate us all with his newly acquired knowledge."

" The poet has been doing nothing of the

kind lately, he has been too much and too
painfully occupied with cube roots and
vulgar fractions."

" Ah, then that accounts for your cube-
rooted antipathy to my wisdom, and your
vulgar fractiousness at my wit."

" I must grant you the wit and wisdom of
changing your front very rapidly."

" Not half so rapidly as our old charwoman,
for she can change her ' front ' whilst passing from the kitchen to the hall door."

" Yes, and what a change,' said Caroline,
" from the most unkempt draggle-tail locks
to frizzled-up ringlets of a quite impossible
stiffness ; looking like spiral springs, upon
which that portentous structure, called a
mob-cap, is supported."

" Have you seen the good body about
whom our young people are talking, Dr.
Noulation ? " said Lady Langdale, " she is

certainly a most curious specimen of our sex."

" Irish, of course," said the Doctor. " I know the species very well. Being a bachelor, my servants content themselves with taking their wages, and when there is any real work to do, suggest the necessity of a charwoman to do it. I have found these much despised folk very useful in times of flagrant servile rebellion, when by a coalition amongst themselves, the servants desert *en masse*, with the amiable intention of putting me to the utmost possible inconvenience. In such times of ' change of ministry' the Irish charwoman forms a useful provisional government."

" What you look upon as merely a ' provisional government, is the established form with us, and very droll and rather inconvenient we found it at first."

"I dare say—I dare say you did; but really you must have a treasure; could anything be more excellently served than the *petit souper* we have just enjoyed?"

"Oh, my girls take charge of all the lighter matters of the *cuisine.*"

"Yes, and we like it so much, dear Doctor," said Caroline. "We have learnt to do so many curious little dishes since we have been here, that it is quite interesting."

"Yes; and why not, my dear young ladies? Cookery is but a branch of my delightful science of chemistry, and requires, in its way, quite as much skill of hand and refinement of touch as the most delicate synthesis of the laboratory."

"With this manifest advantage, that its results are more immediately pleasing, and, perhaps, even more remotely advantageous to the personal happiness," said Gilbert.

" Hardly the latter," said Sir Geoffrey, " if
what I hear about your doings is true,
Doctor. I am told that you have already
discovered a new power, which is to revolu-
tionize society, pay off the national debt,
bring about the Millennium—"

" And ruin the discoverer ! "

" Yes, quite true; especially the last part
of the report; but seriously, Sir Geoffrey, is
not your Government a strange one ? It
fosters, with most lavish encouragement, and
rewards with its highest prizes, the lawyer-
class, *i.e.*, the men who have lived and thriven
upon the strifes and crimes of their fellow-
men, and whose highest avowed aims have
been always to make the worse, appear the
better, cause. It endeavours its utmost to
ennoble by knighthood or baronetcies Mi Lord
Maires, whose capacities are chiefly capacities
for turtle and champagne, and whose grandest

achievement is to ' bore ' some king or prince
with a ponderous banquet; and having thus
exhausted the fountain of honour, it has
none to spare for the encouragement or reward of those amongst us who devote lives
and fortunes to the highest problems of life,
and the greatest needs of mankind."

" Encouragement ! reward ! My dear
Doctor, have you been for a trip into Utopia?
How else could you have conceived the pre-
posterous idea, that either a Government or a
people would give the reward of rank or
wealth to the pioneers of social advance-
ment? Have you forgotten Aristides—ostra-
cised for being too just; Socrates, poisoned
for being too wise; Columbus sent back in
fetters to the old world for discovering the
new; Galileo tortured for revealing the laws
of the planets; and One crucified for mani-
festing the will of God! Shall we, then, mere

pigmy descendants of the Doers and the Re-
vealers of old—doing and revealing, as we
may, such tasks and such secrets as God has
given us to do and to know—shall we expect, in our degree, smoother paths, happier
fates, better rewards than the world had in
store for our forerunners? No! no! dear
Doctor; let us have our grumble now and
then; 'tis an Englishman's privilege, which
I willingly share with you, even, though you
are a Frenchman; but in our heart of hearts
you know, as well as I can tell you, we,
neither of us, expect honour or reward from
the wisdom of a Government, or the gratitude of a people. We can, and must extort
enough for our needs by other labours than
our highest, but the highest work is always
the least rewarded."

"It is so in literature, even I, with my
very young experience, can testify," said

Gilbert. " My epics, into which I poured my whole soul, revelling in the sacrifice of summer days and sleepless nights, supported by the glad hope that many might read them and rejoice; these, despite the warm and genial praise of the few, are *caviare* to the many; whilst hack-work prose, which I despise, even as I write it; trumpery lyrics with little dainty fancies in them, are now my best resources for increasing the store of our little common-wealth."

Pierce had listened with an expression of some pain and perplexity to these bitter truths; for they put before him vividly two possible careers in life—one a high and noble task into which a man might fling his whole life and health, and stake them willingly on the up-cast; and another career of quiet accumulative gainings; not wrong in themselves; indeed, right and wise, with a right and honourable purpose in view ; but for the time, and in the gaining, somewhat distasteful and ignoble. All this passed through his brain vaguely, as the other men were speaking, and yet with sufficient coherence to produce an uneasiness, and a feeling of irresolution and doubt in his mind.

Joining in the conversation, he said—" Do you think it well for us younger men, who have to fight our way to a position in the world, that we also should have two tasks in hand simultaneously ? Should we not rather devote our undivided energies to the making of our fortunes, and afterwards to the higher aim of spending them wisely ? "

" When the struggle is severe and protracted, and when it is a hand-to-hand tussel, with Want on one side of the gulf and Man on the other, each tugging at the rope, why then, decidedly, you had better not waste your

strength in writing epics, or following out
deep researches; but directly you have pulled
Want into the gulf, and can haul away at the
rope without fear of being tugged in yourself, it is then policy, as well as duty, to take
breath, and give an occasional glance up at
the stars; for the stars, looking down as they
do through all eternity upon the toils of
humanity, inspire those toils with higher
motives than can be found on earth; and
whilst they seem to gaze into our very eyes, as
though they would read our thoughts, they
ask us with a voice, like that of conscience.
What is it ye are doing? for what are ye working? and what will be the end of all the
labour with which ye are labouring?

If to these questions, which are as audible
to the soul as yonder passing-bell is to the
ear, we can only reply, 'I want smarter
clothes, a bigger and better furnished house,

larger grounds, more horses, carriages, and servants;' I'm afraid we shall soon be rather ashamed of looking up to our bright little questioners; or probably revenge ourselves for these inconvenient interrogatories by getting a smattering of astronomy, and calling them bad names."

" I pity the man," said Gilbert, " who can smirkingly wink up at the glorious starlit vault, and glibly gabble away all its wonder and beauty by counting off its constellations on his fingers."

" Yes, and flatter himself that he knows all about the stars because he can classify them into little, less, least, or big, bigger, biggest."

" Ah, but it will not do to despise classification," said Dr. Noulaiton, " 'tis the first step out of the Chaos of Ignorance."

" True; but one may despise those who

are content to make only the first step; it is
this smug contentment with small dabblings
into many sciences that gives us so many
self-conceited prigs, who, because they have
learnt a few grand-sounding words out of the
Vocabulary of Science, fondly imagine that
they have mastered the science itself."

" 'Tis a curious hallucination, shared in
some measure by men far above mere dab-
blers."

" Yes, when men have given a name to a
thing they imagine they know what it is."

" Could anything in reality be much more
absurd! We call certain inexplicable pheno-
mena ' Electricity,' but do we know in the
slightest degree what Electricity is ? "

" We know its effects, and we know what
causes will produce those effects, but of itself,
—absolutely nothing ; the strangeness and the
mystery of the existence of such a power in

the earth are not abolished by giving it a name."

"Nor even by observing and recording its effects."

"No! the essence and first cause of gravitation, for example, is as completely beyond our ken as if neither Galileo, Copernicus or Newton had ever existed. We know, of course, that a large mass attracts a little one; but the everlasting 'Why?' is as much hidden from man as it was in the beginning—and of first causes we know no more than Adam."

"Is not gravitation rather too ponderous a subject, dear papa, for us poor ignorant girls to carry in our heads?"

"Perhaps it is, Milly; although a little gravity now and then, at *very* long intervals, would not be wholly undesirable in your case."

"If Mildred has ventured to pass from

grave to gay, I hope you will not go from 'lively to severe,' Geoffrey."

"That is rather severe of you, my dear wife, for I am certainly conscious that our conversation was anything but lively; so let us revert to the lighter matters which, because they are close to us, look so very large."

"Like the blue-bottle on the object-glass of a telescope, which looks big enough to devour the sun."

"Oh, pray don't get back to the heavenly bodies, or we shall be all star-gazing again directly."

"I sit corrected, Miss Mildred; it is, of course, very natural that the stars of earth should be just a trifle jealous of the stars of heaven."

"And yet they are so near to us that surely they need fear no rivalry."

" Certainly not, at your age, Pierce," retorted the Doctor. " Nor at mine either," he
added, *sotto voce.*

" So, Mr. Falconer," said Caroline, " it is
only nearness that enables you philosophers
to see us. We feel flattered in being looked
upon as blue-bottles in a telescope, flutter-
ing about and obscuring your view of the
sun."

" Poor insect," said Gilbert; " but why do
you buzz so wrathfully at ' Poor Pierce?'
It was not he who drove the fly into the telescope."

" Rather a difficult feat, that," quoth Sir
Geoffrey. " We have heard of driving a
four-in-hand through an Act of Parliament;
but the driving a fly into a telescope was a
conception reserved for the vivid imagination
of Mr. Gilbert Langdale."

" If I may be heard in my own defence,

Miss Langdale, allow me to say that I had no conception of comparing you to a fly."

" Not even a butterfly?" asked Mildred.

" Only so far as the butterfly is taken as the type of the soul."

" Thank you very much," said Miss Langdale, rising and making him a profound curtsey; " but I have no pretension to be all soul."

" No, indeed," thought Pierce, " thou art the fairest body that ever stood upon the earth in the light of the sun."

" No," said Gilbert, aloud; " we are quite aware that you are somebody of very great consequence."

" Is that meant as a compliment or an impertience, Mr. Gilbert?"

" However it was meant, I would advise you to take it as a compliment, my fair sister. Always put the pleasantest inter-

pretation upon whatever is said to you;
'tis a mild philosophy, and an eminently
agreeable one."

"Dear me!" said Mildred. "How long
is it since you have turned Solon? And do
you practise your own philosophy when the
critics faintly praise your poems?"

"The girls are too many for you, Gilbert,"
laughed Sir Geoffrey. "In a contest with
silks and satins a man is sure to be
worsted."

It will be noticed that Pierce took little
part in this small badinage with which the
others amused themselves, for, indeed, the
silly fellow had neither eyes, nor ears, nor
tongue for any thing or any one but *la belle*
Caroline, and although he contrived to hide
this infatuation from others, I could see
plainly that he wished us all at the—well—
the Antipodes, so that he might have a few

precious minutes of uninterrupted converse with that young lady.

The longed-for opportunity came at last, for when we rose to leave, the evening was so warm that the girls and Gilbert accompanied us as far as the stables from which the coach started, and where our horses were stalled. Gilbert paired off with Dr. Noulaiton, I took Mildred, and Pierce, Caroline. And then? Oh, then was told again that sweet true tale of ever faithful love—the stronger, the purer, the fairer for all fires of pain, and separation, and fear, and grief that it had passed through. Not many words are needed for that tale—'tis one that goes without much telling—a gentle pressure of hand on arm, a deep long look into the loved eyes—and—all is told; lips are made for other purposes as well as that of speech, and silence itself is often the sweetest eloquence.

Has any one observed, under circumstances
similar to those I have just mentioned, how
very, very often, certain young people shake
each other by the hand and say good-bye
before the really last hand-shake and the inevitable and final "good-bye" is finally
accomplished?

First, in the cottage itself, where, in a fit
of absence, and forgetting wholly that
Caroline was coming with us, Mr. Pierce
thought it needful to go through this
ceremony; then at the end of the lane,
when it was being debated whether they
should walk further or return, another impressive leave-taking was quite innocently
improvised; then, at the entrance of the
stable-yard, a third was imperative, and then,
as we came forth, leading our horses to that
entrance before mounting, another; and
finally, when once fairly in the saddle, all

former farewells were evidently entirely forgotten in the quietly-sad fervour of this.
Nor did it quite end here, for in mere courtesy
we were bound to escort our fair hostesses
back to their Cottage, and again and at last,
for the *absolute last time*, the electric contact of hand, and flash of eyes, was reluct-
antly broken and lost.

The evening was simply delicious after the
heat of a summer noon. The fresh
fragrance of earth and her flowers rose into
the calm moonlit air, and hovered round us
like invisible fairies, touching our senses with
subtle and indescribable delights. A trans-
parent illuminated mist gave an ethereal
beauty to field and trees, and softened all the
harsher outlines of roadway, roof, or wall.
The strongly-contrasted colours of glaring day
were blended into a soft and graduated
harmony that rested and charmed the eye,

whilst the coolness that came and gently fanned us in the face, as we rode, refreshed and invigorated us, and brought with it the power of enjoyment for all the sights and sounds that greeted eye and ear.

This much abused world is indeed still very beautiful; filled by its beneficent Creator with wondrous charms and ever-changing aspects of loveliness, needing only the finer attuning of our own hearts to make it seem a veritable heaven; and from what seemingly prosaic sources pleasure pours into our souls. The sharp clear-cut line of a gabled roof distinctly yet softly defined against the blue sky; the splash and foam of a mill stream or the quieter ripple of the river; the arch of a bridge, the distant broken music of a peal of bells, the moonlight through the leaves, or on the stems of trees, or streaming away over the meadows till lost in the mysterious dark-

ness of the far-off forest; the tinkle of a
sheep-bell, the bay of a watch-dog, and, more
than all, the rich full notes of mavis, merle,
and nightingale, all these pleasures come
flowing in upon us many times in our lives,
but at no time with such a joyous rush of
gladness as when the heart is touched by the
great magician—" Love."

We did not speak of these things to each
other as we rode on our way, because to
catalogue what one sees, or hears, or feels, is
simply to crush out all its beauty; a mere
chatter-pie, at such a time, is one of the dis-
cords of life ; a fellow who says, " oh, look
there !" " oh, see yonder," " oh, hear that,"
or " oh, hark to t'other," and " oh, how nice
and fresh," and " oh, how sweet the flowers
smell," " oh, this," and " oh, that," through
the whole string of delightful pleasures that
are filling you with a silent joy and an un-

speakable gratitude, is one of the greatest nuisances in the whole creation, and one feels inclined to "brain" the shallow chatterer with my lady's fan. Such things refuse to be inventoried, and "ticked off," they are too fine and too delicate to be put into interjections, and at the sound of a coarse and careless mortal voice they vanish, like spirits, into thin air. Alas, they vanish all too fast, even without the disenchanting voice. It is not possible to keep our senses highly strung for any great length of time, and without that first high tension, we soon get out of tune with nature and relapse into prosaic discord. Who has not turned away from the finest scene ever presented to him with a vague feeling that he has drunk in a great draught of beauty, but that it is gone; that it can never again be enjoyed with its first freshness, that it is a book that is read, a picture seen, a joy

enjoyed ?   Else why do we always turn away
from it with a sigh and never turn to it without a disappointment ?   No, as Byron has
well said, " This flesh will sink immortal
spirits," and the sting of a gnat, the twinge
of a toothache, or a touch of cramp pulls us
down out of fairy-land with frightful rapidity.

Happily none of these trivialities came to
break our dreams of beauty that night, and
for a long time we rode silently over
the turf towards Woodford, feeling like two
veritable knights-errant passing through an
enchanted land.   Of course on such a night
it would have been hideously detestable to
ride back into the grim, close city, with its
pavements still hot from the sun, and its
houses giving back to the hours of night
the heat they had absorbed in the day ; hence
moved by a common impulse, we took the
shortest track on to the broad plains of the

Lea, and crossing these at the gallop, gained
the country lane that leads under over-arching
trees, until, like a river, losing itself in the
sea, it opens out into the broad expanse of
forest glade. Tempted by the beauty of the
forest, we still rode on and on, now through a
narrow bridle path, where we had to take
Indian file, anon coming to broad open plains,
stretching away in many directions, but
nothing tempted us aside from our unspoken,
but common impulse, which was to ride to
Wolfern Chace. Almost before we were
aware, we had ridden softly up the avenue
and had drawn rein in the fore-court, gazing,
with many memories in our eyes, at the windows where many a glad sight had been seen,
and many a sweet face had looked forth. The
whole front lay in the full soft splendour of the
moonlight, and reflected back the radiance
with a clearness like that of day, but whilst

we were thus enjoying this part of our midnight dream, we were suddenly awakened by
the throwing up of a window, the protrusion
of a blunderbuss, and the tones of a cracked
voice shouting, " What be yeow men arter
theer?" Attracted by the sounds, we recognized
the grimy visage of the old gardener, surmounted first by a white night-cap, and then
by an old beaver hat of Sir Geoffrey's; a
world too wide for the present wearer, and
placed on his head at an angle of forty-five
degrees, to prevent it from falling over his
eyes. Our amusement at this figure of fun
was tempered by a natural distaste for
the contents of the blunderbuss, whatever
they might be, and so we hastily assured
the grim guardian that we had come on
no felonious intent ; and telling him our
names, asked him if he did not remember
us. He was only too glad to do so, for

the recognition enabled him to resume
sufficient control over himself to restrain his
teeth from chattering so uncomfortably, but,
in drawing back his blunderbuss and his
head simultaneously, the big hat caught on
the edge of the open window, and being thus
disturbed from its position, fell forward over
his face and extinguished him *in toto*. All
his former fears returned in full force, and
judging that he had been assaulted suddenly
from behind, he blazed away with his blunderbuss (happily in the direction of the moon
rather than the earth), and uttered half-
smothered cries of " Murder ! help ! Joe !
thieves ! " At this catastrophe we were now
free to laugh with a mirth unalloyed by
doubts of the blunderbuss, and our laughter
was not lessened by the sudden apparition of
the redoubtable Joe cautiously approaching
up a side path, dodging into the shade as he

came along. When he, also recognizing us, emerged into the full splendour of the moonlight, we saw that in his haste and nervousness he had mistaken his smock frock for his trousers, and with an ingenuity and perseverance worthy of a better cause, had succeeded in pulling his thin shanks into the sleeves of that misplaced garment. When we had sufficiently recovered voice to make him aware of this fact, he joined chorus with us in the fun of the thing, and shouting to "Daddy" (as he somewhat disrespectfully designated his venerable parent), assured him it was "all right," and that he had better get into bed again. Whereupon we had the satisfaction of seeing Daddy's face slowly emerge from under its extinguisher, and Daddy himself shut his window and follow his son's advice. Leaving a crown piece for each of them as a solatium for our unintentional disturbance, we rode away with considerably more fun and less romance about us than we had brought down.

Our horses seemed to understand our changed mood, for they began to take a pull at their bits, and to trot out springily as we defiled back through the bridle-path, not un-frequently putting our hats in jeopardy from the low growth of the pollard-oaks, or the large straggling hawthorns and wild roses. When we reached the long, open stretch of forest plain they shook their heads, gave a merry demi-volt, and sailed us away at a fair racing gallop over the springy turf, as if they enjoyed it as much as their riders. I can answer for the latter; there are few things in this world more wholesomely ex-hilarating, or more thoroughly enjoyable than the feeling of a gay horse under you, with

lots of "go" and power to spare, bounding
away with a long loping stride, and keeping
you well neck and neck, or just half a
length a-head of either a friend or a foe
equally well mounted; and perhaps, until,
in the course of development, we obtain
wings, this is the nearest approximation to a
pleasant "fly" that a man can experience.
Then, as we sobered down and drew rein to a
steadier pace through the quaint lanes of
Walthamstow, a thin streak of roseate gold
and ruby opened in the horizon, the breeze
freshened and rustled in the leaves; sleepy
twitterings and chirpings slowly developed
into a full chorus of bird notes—thousands
of the lesser creatures in God's great universe
awoke from the short sleep of their short
lives, as if unwilling to waste one precious
moment of their little day; and all earth's
early risers shook off the mimic death of

night to rejoice in the first delicious rays of the morning sun; for now, with rapid burst, those rays came forth, sending their arrows over the level, and touching with a dazzling glory, tree and river, and transforming many a homely casement into a mirror, sparkling with gems. Slowly and slowly paled the moon, and more and more jocund rose the songs of the birds as our horses broke into the gallop again across the broad marsh-land that forms the valley of the Lea, so that by the time we had forded the river, and gained the road leading through Lower Homerton, it was full daylight.

" 'Tis a pity," said Pierce, " that folks do not know how delicious these early summer mornings are. Men certainly waste a good third of their little lives by too much bed."

" Or, rather, by bed at the wrong time. If I were a despotic king, I would certainly

revive the Curfew for the summer time, and my
subjects would have cause of infinite thank-
fulness to me for the revival."

" It certainly does seem an infatuation
that we should prefer the midnight-oil to the
morning sun, but I suppose, by force of
habit, one always seems more able to do
to think, and to say things at night than in
the morning."

" Especially if the things said are soft
nothings—eh, Pierce ? "

" Well, yes—it would want a great deal
more courage to make a proposal before breakfast than after supper."

" Dutch courage fortified with champagne;
'tis only when the wine's in that the wit's
out; and only when the wit's out that a man
makes a proposal."

" Thank you for the compliment. I judge
from that small bit of sarcasm you inferred

that I did not lose the chance of renewing my suit to *la belle* Caroline last night ? "

" I not only inferred, but I knew it, for you have been as portentously silent ever since, as if you had uttered your whole self, once and for all, in that declaration ; like a bee that in stinging leaves his sting."

" Thank you, once more, for that stinging simile, but the metaphor is a little hazy—is it not ? "

" Never mind, so long as it stings."

" Oh, sting away, as much as you like, for I am armed so strong in happiness, that I would defy a whole beehive to hurt me."

" Dear, brave boy ! you have already hurled a grander defiance at Fate, for in contemplating matrimony you have challenged a hornet's nest of cares."

" You're a cynic; at least, you sham cynicism to cover one of the softest hearts that ever beat at the sight of a pretty face or a trim ancle."

"Thanks for small mercies. I'm glad you didn't accuse me of a soft head."

"*Cela va sans dire.*"

"Hem! you're polite."

"But confess, are you not avowedly in love with at least three pretty women in every season?"

"Of course I am. What were pretty women made for, if we are not to fall in love with them? but there's safety in numbers; like the Irishman in the old song—

"'Sure whenever I try
To get one in my heart I get two in my eye.'"

"Yes, I suppose you think there's luck in odd numbers?"

"Of course; there's no practice equal to the rule of three."

" I suppose you have the effrontery to intend that for an arithmetical pun ? "

" No, it is only a figure of speech."

" Well now, be sensible, if you can, and tell me how it is you do not take a wife ? "

" Because, sir, as was very pensively remarked by a friend of mine, when advised to do so—' I would willingly but then the husbands make such a bother.' "

" Sheridan's answer was better than that— he meekly and deferentially enquired, 'Whose wife shall I take, sir ? ' but do hold hard," continued Pierce, " and don't tempt me to cap any more of your venerable jests; be serious, if you can, and aid me (like a good fellow) to carry out a little plot for Caroline's pleasure. She told me last evening that she and Mildred had the strongest desire to see the Chace again. You remember that when the ruin fell on them they were away travel-

ling, and Sir Geoffrey, thinking to spare
them the heart-ache of a sorrowful leave-
taking of their loved home, so arranged
matters that they never returned to it, but
at once took up their abode where they now
live."

" Was it so ?   I had forgotten ; yes, then it
is of course very natural they should have a
great longing to see the old place.   Well,
what is your project ? "

"Just this.   You give me a mount again
some day, and your company also, and I'll
get some well-trained ladies' horses for the
girls,   and   an   open   carriage   for   Lady
Langdale, Sir Geoffrey,   and   Noulaiton,
and will have a delightful little picnic in
the grounds and a good ramble over the old
house."

" Charming.   I'm   with   you   any   day

you like, but, on one condition, that I divide the charge of this little affair with you."

"Kind as ever! but I ought not to let you, since you lend me your horse and your company, and solely for my pleasure."

"Mine, too, old fellow; I shall enjoy it immensely, 'twill be a pleasant little return for their reception of us yesterday; when shall it be?"

"Oh, not too soon. I'm an epicurean about pleasures of this kind; I don't like to dash through them and then have nothing to look forward to; besides, the planning and arranging all the minor matters will involve not a few calls and consultations for which afterwards there would not be so good an excuse."

"You're a cunning, cold-blooded rascal, if ever there was one! So young and so de-

praved, who could have believed it of
you! I'll have to forswear your company,
or you'll corrupt my young and innocent
mind."

"Shut up," retorted Pierce; "it has come
to a pass when *you* sham innocence. But
you're a jolly good fellow, all the same, and
now here we are at the stables; shall I knock
up old Joe, or shall we just put the horses
away ourselves, they're quite cool, and their
late suppers, or early breakfasts, are sure to
be ready in their mangers."

We did as Pierce suggested, rather than
disturb my faithful old groom, and then, after
a mild glass of wine and a biscuit, we separated
for two or three hours' sleep; but I lingered
long before drawing down the blinds, for
my bedroom window overlooked the river
—the grand old Thames—and the soft, deli-

cious light of the sun came glancing over the waters like a stream of gladness and hope.

The tide was at the full, and just on the turn, and as I stood watching, my thoughts floated outwards, and mingled with the seafarers, who were hauling at their anchors and letting out their sails, and gliding down and away to distant lands.

I wondered if those fine hardy fellows, full of energy and courage, ready to go anywhere, and to dare and do anything, had not found the parting with some kind old mother, some fair young sweetheart, some dear, devoted wife, or some tender, loving child—the hardest thing to do and dare in all the world —and if they, with their manly pride, their strong wills, and responsible duties to enable them to bear up against such griefs, can hardly restrain a tear, or control the choking sensation in the throat—what tears and aching hearts, aching from an utter void, do they leave behind them.

Oh God, have pity " on all those who go down to the sea in ships," and pity with a still more infinite pity those who are left to mourn.

CHAPTER III.

FOLLOWING up the tactics so un-
blushingly avowed, Mr. Pierce be-
came a very frequent visitor at the Cottage,
and with the apparently tacit consent of Sir
Geoffrey and Lady Langdale, the young Jack-
anapes gradually came to look upon himself
as ultimately certain of his prize.

And what a prize it was that thus inspired
his delighted hopes !

Adversity is a fine test for proving the true
gold, and distinguishing it from mere social
lacquer.

'Tis very easy for young ladies to be bright

and graceful, full of spirit, wit and cheerfulness, when all the surroundings of their
lives are pleasant and prosperous ; it is easy
to be exceedingly charming and elegant when
leaning back in a well-appointed barouche—
the centre of attraction, and the object of de-
votion to a group of gay cavaliers ; but when
that same charm of manner, that same in-
born spirit and sunny nature come out as
freshly and delightfully in the performance
of unaccustomed, and not pleasing duties, and
the same bright, loving nature is shown
amidst the daily troubles, cares and crosses
of a life of severe retrenchment and humble
position ; then it is that the real character is
really revealed, and in that revelation be-
comes doubly dear and loveable.

It was simply delightful to note how these
two young girls quite naturally and unconsciously took up their new and strange parts

in the poor little home, and how Caroline especially, found, without seeking or effort, that the uses of adversity are, indeed, sweet, when rightly used.

After Pierce's first unsuccessful proposal it was not in woman's nature to avoid a saddened and somewhat disappointed tone of thought and feeling which could not fail to make itself more or less apparent; but when the heavy, universal sorrow came—and came with such a crushing blow upon her father—she hid away her own private grief so effectually as to become the most cheerful of the whole little circle. Possibly those ruthless anatomists of human motives, who delight in mental vivisection, might sneeringly point out to us that this restored cheerfulness was from the forecast that Pierce would not now be so far apart from her in station.

Well, Cynic, suppose we grant that this

had its influence as a part motive, why need
we ignore the other and still nobler causes of
this change? Do we not all act, at almost all
times, from mixed motives, and why need we
expend so much acuteness in discovering and
parading the lower, rather than the higher,
springs of action?

You, sir or madam, have the reputation for
immense profundity, marvellous insight into
character; you have, beyond all cavil, a very
large share of double-cunning in your com-
position, and occasionally see more things in
heaven and earth than ever were there:
hence it is your especial delight, as showman
or showwoman of what is the cant of the day
to call "Vanity Fair" to pick out the
shakiest characters you can find, and attri-
bute all their actions to the lowest motives;
aye, even though clearer and brighter reasons
for such actions are on the surface, and open

to the light of day, still you must show your
depth by dabbling your pens down into the
dregs and stirring up the mud. Well, well,
you know your trade; you write books to
sell, and the world is very impatient at being
told of people better than itself; on the
contrary, it experiences a smug satisfaction
in hearing of those who are worse, Perfectly
natural! You know human nature well, and
turn your knowledge to good account. For
example, in one novel, a perfectly impossible
Man-about-Town figures as the chief attraction, whose actions and impulses are utterly
abominable. Thereupon the absolute and
living Sir Mulberry Hawk flings away
the book with a "Hang it, I'm bad
enough; but, by Jove, I'm not so bad as
that!" and he feels quite virtuous by com-
parison with his caricature; or Lady Loosely,
turning languidly over the pages where a

demirep of the dirtiest water is the heroine,
says—" ah, how dreadful! did you ever?"
And she also has a temporary attack of virtuous indignation very gratifying to her very
dubious reputation.

Again, old Mr. Midas Hard-Cash, seeking
a short relaxation from the bargains of the
day, reads a graphic description of the un-
mitigated villainies of a fictitious usurer, and
thereupon plumes himself, like a sleek pouter-
pigeon, "thanking God that he is not as
other men are."

This peculiarity of human nature, ex-
plains the popularity of books which treat of
the various wickednesses of life, rather
than its virtues; and accounts for the
far deeper interest which children show for
the bad boys and bad girls of their stories
rather than the good ones.

Knowing this, why do I forsake the obvious high-road to popularity and travel by preference through the narrow paths of truth, where so few will care to follow me? Simply because I do not write for grown-up children, but for men and women, many of the best of whom are heartily sick of looking at the night-side of Nature, and would fain be refreshed by seeing that poor humanity, with all its weakness and error, is yet capable of doing its world-work fairly and cheerfully, even under trying circumstances.

So, at least, and, in very truth, did all my well-loved friends at the Cottage; therefore, dear reader, if you are yearning for a little highly-spiced impropriety, or fascinating wickedness, go to the nearest circulating library; and even though it be but in a little village or a country town, you can get your choice of as much villainy in three volumes as would almost be the justification for another deluge.

The sunny cheerfulness which had at first been so gracefully assumed, was now, indeed, as natural and real as that of a bird which sings as it flies, from the mere joyousness of life; sings, not because it ought to sing, but because the sun shines, and the heavens are blue and clear; because the fresh breezes buoy it up, and its wings rejoice in their strength; because the lawns are fresh and green, and the flowers are bright and fragrant; because, in a word, Earth is Earth, and not a Hell.

Nay, and not only so; for the time had come again to Caroline Langdale when Earth seemed almost Heaven; for had not Pierce, in the deep, earnest tones of truth, told her of his unswerving, all-absorbing love for her; how the thought of her sweet smile had

nerved him through days of disappointment
and nights of watching; how the hope yet to
win for her a position and fit place in life had
made the hardest tasks light, and the severest
studies easy; and how her image was like
the gentle Madonna-shrine on the dusty high-
way, ever there to give him courage to pursue
his journey; and how the memories of her
words came floating around him on his way
like fairy music?

Sweet to maidens' ear are such confessions
when they come welling up from the heart—
albeit, in broken utterances, well-nigh stopped
by their very eagerness to get themselves
uttered. How unlike such plain and rugged
confessions are to the little meandering, thin
streams of shallow compliment, babbling
fluently along into every fair ear in turn,
with an undertone of vanity and conceit in
their own babblings; and trust a woman's

wit for quickly discerning the difference, and estimating each at its true value. It was a crowning mercy for Sir Geoffrey that his wife and daughters had brought their sunshine with them into the lowly home, for now had commenced a hard fight for both himself and Gilbert, each in their several ways. For himself, the scientific investigation into new powers of nature and art, which he had commenced with the hope of doing a large public service, had even in his time of wealth been a heavy strain upon his resources, and through many long years he had denied him-self all personal indulgences, so that he might be justified in carrying out large and costly experiments.

The result of these experiments had been watched with great and increasing interest by a large and wide-spread circle of scientific and intellectual men, and had been regularly recorded by the Press at each new stage of progress. His system, in its progressive developments, had been adopted and followed with some success both in England and abroad, but, of course, without any pecuniary advantage to himself.

Equally, of course, this circumstance had not been a matter of disappointment to him; this had been a labour of love, and, however Quixotic it may sound, I believe he loved his self-imposed task infinitely better, and laboured at it with a higher pleasure, because he had never intended, and never expected, to make money by it.

There are some old-fashioned folk, simple-minded and weak enough to crave some world-work that has not money for its object; something to do that involves a fair and healthful exercise of daily and yearly self-sacrifice; and Sir Geoffrey, with all his knowledge of the world and society, with all his contempt for the cant of philanthrophy, and distrust of blind head-over-heels enthusiasms, was yet one of those foolish, unworldly people.

It can therefore be dimly understood that the double necessity which now compelled him to relinquish all further costly experiments, and, to endeavour to obtain some addition to his scanty income from his foregone labours, was like a sharp cord binding his arms to his side and pulling him two ways at once; and such fettering was the more painful because his system had now arrived at the tantalising point when a few more bold and dashing sorties into the realms of the "unknown" would have climaxed and completed the discovery. These would have involved the risk of some thousands, and Sir Geoffrey now grudged even the expenditure of a single sovereign, forasmuch as it lessened by so much the

already small resources for his " home-birds."
To say that these now saved, and stinted
themselves in all the quiet little ways
possible; not parading their economies, but
taking quite as much pains to conceal as to
concert them, is merely to say that they were
women with their hearts in the right place;
but, none the less, Sir Geoffrey saw through
and through their kind little devices, and
daily registered a vow to work to the bitter
end, and by all possible means, with the hope
of some day showing them how warmly he
appreciated their sacrifices.

His vow was not altogether a superfluous
one; for the days as they came heavily up,
one after one, brought many " bitter ends " to
many bright hopes, and called forth all his
resolution and philosophy; but, happily, resolution and philosophy strengthen with use,
and if a man shows a cheerful face and a

brave front to the troubles of life, it's quite amusing to see how these troubles slink away, like snarling curs, with their tails betwixt their legs. Still the snarling curs are not pleasant antagonists, especially when they persist in snapping at one's heels on every possible occasion, or when they assume the guise of that proverbial wolf, which it is traditionally difficult to keep from the door. However, by self-denial on the part of each and all, that unpleasant animal was kept out for a time.

CHAPTER IV.

"WHAT a queer, proud fellow that brother of mine is," said William Langdale to his wife, as they sat cosily together in their luxurious dining-room, with an elaborate dessert upon the table, flanked by fabulously old "comet" port and magnificent brown sherry. "What a very extraordinary fellow, Ann, I say! Eh?"

"My dear," said the lady, somewhat emphatically, at the same time delicately champing an almond with teeth as white and pearly as the almond itself, "My dear, I can quite understand that with his fine nature he could never consent to be your pensioner, or even to accept a loan from you, if he could possibly do without it; and I respect and love him all the better for it."

"But why, why, why? Condemn it! Confound it!"

"Hush, William, for shame! for shame, sir!"

"Well, well, you know what I mean. Why should a man refuse to let his own brother lend him a hand when he's tumbled into a ditch? Besides, it isn't as if we had children to provide for; here I've heaps of money idle at my bankers, and have positively to bother my old brains to find out anything new to buy for you. And here's my mother's son—a chap that I used to thrash as I liked when we were boys—stands me out on his dignity, with his reasons and his thanks, and his refusals, till I'm half inclined to see if

I ain't strong enough yet to thrash him again."

"Be quiet, William, do, and don't roar yourself into a fury like an absurd old lion lashing himself with his own tail. You're a dear, good old 'hub' as ever lived, and as generous as good; but don't you remember what quaint Dr. Watts says? 'If your wine be never so good, and you never so liberal with it, if you will persist in pouring it lavishly into a narrow-necked phial, it is sure to be spilt.'"

"Dr. Watts be hanged! Let's see, I think he was, wasn't he? Oh, no, that was Dr. Dodd; ah, it's all the same, they were both Doctors. But what does Dr. Watts know about such things? I'll be bound if he had such a glass of port as this before him, he wouldn't be a narrow-necked phial!"

"No, dear, nor a vial of wrath either, I

dare say; but why should you lift up your
horn and butt the poor old Doctor because I
ventured to quote him?"

"The somebody can quote Scripture when
it serves his purpose."

"Thank you, sir, for the implied com-
parison! But Dr. Watts is not Scripture,
and I'm not 'the somebody.'"

"No, you're an angel, a darling, a beauty.
There never was such a woman as my Nan,
and there never will be again!" said William
Langdale, in a paroxysm of admiration for
his clever wife.

"Now, William, do be sensible for once."

"How can I be sensible to anything but
your perfections, my charmer, my angel?"

"William!" retorted the lady, speaking
with considerable emphasis, "do not be so
silly, but listen to some little plans which I
have formed for helping, without wounding,

your dear brother. First, I have been enquiring for Gilbert's last new poem at every library and bookseller's that I pass in my morning drives, and buying copies wherever they have them. This will make a stir amongst the publishers. Then I have sent these copies to literary men who can, and will understand and appreciate the merit of the work. This will make a stir amongst the critics."

" Well, yes, that will 'tell up' for Gilbert by-and-bye, and give the young fellow a chance of being valued more fairly in future."

" That is all I claim for this part of my project, and this is all that can or should be fairly done ; I use no favouritism, no influence. I merely write and say to my friends *there* is the book ; if you like it, speak of it and say so. If you don't, say why you don't, and both the author and myself will thank you for pointing out its faults."

" I don't understand much about criticism, but I don't think that's how it's done as a rule."

" No; certainly not, and yet until it is so done, it will continue to be looked upon with doubt and suspicion, and gradually lose more and more of the vast and useful power it might assume and retain. But you, dear old dunce, amidst all your calculations, have you ever considered the splendid chances of a young poet without any literary godfathers or godmothers ? "

" H'm! I shouldn't offer much for those chances on 'Change."

" I don't suppose you would; and I shouldn't be much elated if I drew them as a prize out of a shilling raffle. Listen; his work comes out, and wins its first success by exciting three or four columns of virulent abuse in the leading satirical review of the day. Slowly, but surely, this violent vituperation brings its reaction, and after a while, unbiassed, impartial critics reverse the verdict, and welcome it with honest and genial praise."

"Well, that's all right. Then the work is sure to be popular, and everybody will buy it."

"You dear old credulous John Bull! Not a bit of it; you know I have simply described the reception of Gilbert's book, and what is the result? Why, his publishers tell him they do not sell twenty copies a year!"

"Swindlers! They must sell them, and pocket the proceeds!"

"A great many hot-headed young poets share your view; but you are all wrong. Barabbas may have been a publisher, but I don't think all publishers are Barabbases; and there is no occasion to maintain that theory in order to account for the fact. There are a great many other facts about this question; first, there's not one in ten thousand of prosy English folk who really cares a straw for poetry. Next, of that minute minority, a great many will beg a book; a great many more will borrow; a select few, will steal; but not one in a thousand will buy it; and he,—that *rara avis* himself, will generously lend it to all his friends, instead of bidding them go and do likewise."

"Ah well, when other trades fail I don't think I'll be a poet."

"I don't think you will ; but you need not fret about it, because you couldn't if you would."

"What, not with the inspiration of your eyes, my charmer, my angel? I could do Romeo to your Juliet to perfection."

"Nonsense, William, you're too fat; and

you interrupt me in what I want to say
There! there! be quiet, you old goose,
and go to your own side of the table again!
Let me see. What was I saying?"

"Well, you were trying to hoax me into
the belief that, however well reviewed a
poet's work may be, no one will buy it, and
therefore if he is poor to begin with, he stands
a fine chance of being considerably poorer for
his pains."

"Just so; like honesty in the proverb, he
is praised and starved. A favourable review
is barely a nine days' wonder; and even the
twenty or thirty of these, speaking in highest
praise of Gilbert's work have had scarcely any
effect 'commercially' as you City men say."

"Well then, I say again, his publishers are
'doing him.' They have printed twice the
number arranged for, and are selling their
part of the plunder first."

"Nonsense William! look round the libraries and drawing-rooms of our wide circle of friends and acquaintances, and where do you really find *new* books? Standard works in plenty, with magnificent bindings—and unopened pages; well-thumbed novels from Sam's or Mitchell's; occasionally a volume of a very fashionable and delightfully improper poet; and the very latest roarings of the very largest lion, of course; but of the young fresh thought of the age, expressed in the highest form, there is no sign or token any-where. I believe there is nothing about which even the richest people are so mean and niggardly as in the purchase of books?"

"Why should we give pounds and shillings for what we can borrow for pence?"

"Because a poem, if it is worth reading once, is worth reading a dozen times. That which has taken a finely-attuned mind years

to utter, cannot be comprehended in a day.
There are delicacies and subtleties of music
and meaning, exquisite little pictures, and
happy turns of thought in any fine poem, not
one-tenth of which are appreciated or understood at the first reading."

" Oh, thank you ! do you mean to say that
we're to keep spelling over and over again
at the same work, like a child at its horn-
book ? "

" Now it's all very well for you, you great
rough diamond, to pretend to be matter-of-
fact and contradictious, when I have seen you
take up your nephew's book, time after time,
and you have always had to wipe your
spectacles hard when you closed it."

" Ah, well, that's because he's my nephew
you know, and I like the young vagabond, even
though he is fool enough to write poetry."

" Yes, and because one ' touch of nature

makes the whole world kin;' and when now
I come to think that a great, blustering
commonplace, prosaic, dear old bear like
you, can yet be touched by a nobly-
expressed feeling, I recant what I said about
prosy English-folk; and am half inclined to
believe that the sturdiest of John Bulls and
the sternest men of business may possibly
be vulnerable to the same fine influence;
and that if it were only placed within reach
of their hands, it would speedily touch their
hearts."

"You little Jesuit, I see what you have
worked round to. You think that you have
thus excused your disreputable conduct in
assisting surreptiously in the wider distribu-
tion of your favourite's book!"

"I glory in my conduct! I am a heroine!
I have been a benefactress of my race without
being aware of it or intending it!"

"You shameless little imposter—but you're an angel all the same!"

"Well, now you have found such a good excuse for my doings, I confess that at first I was a little ashamed of them, only that I meant to buy up all the books which I had hoaxed the bookselling men to buy, if they did not sell them."

"What a genius was lost to the Stock Exchange when Fate decreed that you should wear petticoats instead of—a-hem——"

"Some people are rude enough to say that I do wear what you are pleased to call the 'a-hem.'"

"Of course you do, my angel-on-horseback, and who could possibly wear them more gracefully?"*

* This was rather a smart hit for William Landgale, for Mrs Langdale was a splendid horsewoman, and faint rumours had found credence that for long rides she really did, literally, as well as metaphorically, assume the garments in question. I believe this is the usual thing, now-a days, but it had all the piquancy of novelty then.

"What a troublesome old tease you are ! Don't you want to know what other little stratagems I have devised?"

"Yes, yes; certainly, certainly, but if I knew how to do it, I've an idea that I could trump your last card with regard to Gilbert."

"Show me your hand; I shall be delighted to be beaten at my own game."

"Well, you see, if one could trust to those rascally publishers, I would put £500 to their credit to be expended by them in announcements of Gilbert's book. He need never know but what they were doing it on their own account."

"Dear old Fuzz! Capital! what a brilliant idea, and you can do it with perfect safety; for, happily, with this last work Gilbert changed his publisher, and his present one is, I am sure, an honest man, for he dissuaded him from his venture, and told him candidly that, however good poetry might be, and however well received by the critics, he absolutely and truly 'did not know of a public,' for that branch of literature."

" Which fact Gilbert has found too true, I suppose?"

" Painfully true, and under his present circumstances very disastrous. He naturally thought that if his work was good enough to run the gauntlet of criticism and come out with flying colours and hearty applause, that it would, in the nature of things, help to win him a little daily bread ; but alack, poor boy, had this been his sole resource, he might, like poor Otway, have starved on Fame and been choked by a penny roll; but although sorely straitened, and still more perplexed and bewildered by this curious state of things, he does not turn down his collars and take to frowning like Byron ;

nor mope himself into a consumption like poor Keats; but locking his MS. in his desk, and his aspiration in his heart, has set manfully to work to earn his living by bright, ephemeral hack-work."

" Ah, he's one of the right sort; and has fortunately inherited a good deal of dogged courage from his father, and still more bright cheerfulness of heart from his mother. I must lend him a helping hand, and pull him through, even at the risk of his finding me out."

" Do, do, dear old hubby, and I'll love you if possible, better than ever! But now I've something else to propose, so just pour me out one glass more sherry, (I have not had my third yet, because we have been so busy talking), and I'll tell you all about my other plan."

The golden wine was poured out, and

daintily sipped, displaying in the action a
white hand of very perfect shape, adorned
with splendid diamond rings, and the lady
then resumed—

" This season I think we had better go to
the Thames; you did not get your usual time
of fishing last year, and I'm sure you missed it.
Well, let us take a good capacious house,
instead of going to hotels, and then we'll have
the girls down first; and we won't let
them go back unless Sir Geoffrey and Lady
Langdale come to fetch them ; and when once
we have inveigled them all down, trust me
for keeping them. Gilbert, of course, can
run down in the evenings, and a certain Mr.
Pierce Falconer will probably come down
with him ; whereupon Miss Caroline will look
as demure and as unconcerned as any saint,
and yet be as glad in her heart as the veriest
sinner."

"Good ! Do just as you like ; you know I always leave such matters to you."

"Yes, and Mr. Fallington shall come for a short visit, to see if he's improved; and I'll think over ' all sorts and conditions of men,' literary, scientific and ' rich ' who are likely, in any way, to be useful to Sir Geoffrey and Gilbert."

"Well, yes ! But let us have some of our dramatic friends as well, to enliven the others."

"With all my heart ; Liston, and his dear funny little wife have long promised me a visit ; Braham will come, I know ; and my awfully splendid friend, Mrs. Siddons— because I never bore her with making any fuss over her. I shouldn't wonder if she would bring Kean to spend a Sunday with us."

"Capital ; this will put the spirit into our

social punch-bowl. Your scientific friends are apt to be bitter ; your literary men acid ; your millionaires slow and sickly ; but your dramatic folks are always bright and full of fun, like boys and girls just escaped for a holiday."

"To carry out your 'spirited' simile, I suppose you would have said that they contribute the dram because of their (dram) attic salt."

"Oh! you hardened little sinner! that is, indeed, a drop too much; but hadn't you better secure your castle in the air before peopling it ?"

"That is easily done; ring for Perkins and bid him bring the 'Times.' The immortal George Robins is sure to have at least half-a-dozen Paradises to let at this time of the year."

The bell was rung, and the sardonic

Perkins brought the paper, and began to clear the table; Mrs. Langdale hastily glanced down the columns, and then, prefacing with a light, merry laugh, read as follows—

"'On the banks of the pellucid, silvery, cool, paternal Thames! that majestic father of many waters!—'"

"Many daughters, did you say?" enquired William Langdale.

"Waters, sir! Do I read so very indistinctly?" asked his lady, with mock dignity.

"You read like a Siddons, my angel! Go on."

"'Majestic father of many waters; Mr George Robins—'"

"Excuse me, is Mr. George Robins the majestic father of many waters?"

"Dunce!" retorted Mrs. Langdale, whereupon William Langdale winked at Perkins, who suffered a scarcely perceptible twitter to hover at the corner of his mouth.

"'Mr. George Robins has the supreme honour of being permitted to offer to any distinguished family a perfect Paradise! A residence—a garden—and—grounds—upon which wealth, instructed by art, and guided by the hand of taste, has lavished princely adornments. The suites of apartments glide gracefully into one another, blending into one harmonious whole—'"

"What a remarkable performance," said the husband, *sotto voce.*

"'They are furnished with the softest of carpets; the richest and most becoming of curtains; couches upon which merely to recline is a delicious luxury; beds that lull e'en restless cares to sleep!

"'Choicest gems of *bijouterie* and *vertu*

decorate the saloons, and even the mirrors are skilfully adjusted upon scientific principles, to give none but the pleasantest reflections ! '

" 'So much for the mansion itself ; but what pen can do justice to the fairy-like gardens, filled with Hesperian fruits ; the emerald lawns; the shady groves where ' Nymphs might sport, but Satyrs never come.' One feature, alone, in this earthly paradise must ever give it an intense, a sweet interest in the eyes of dignified matrons, with groups of graceful, marriageable daughters, and that is The Lover's Walk, by the brink of the river, in the deep alcoves of which the most eligible proposals have been made, and invariably accepted."

" Quite a family house," said William Langdale, " I wonder Robins did not add— '. Husbands provided on the shortest notice ;'

or 'a large assortment of eligible lovers kept in stock in the neighbourhood ; ' but stop a bit, Mrs. William Langdale—there are ' proposals and proposals,' and there are certain proposals to a certain lady, that I, for one, should *not* consider eligible, and certainly should not wish to be ' invariably accepted.' "

" Oh, if you wish to play the part of the jealous husband, I shall be most happy to oblige."

" Thank you very much—how good of you ! but I don't. ' All-coves ' are not to be trusted ; especially with my wife."

" That is simply the most disgraceful pun I ever heard you utter ; and that is saying something."

" Please 'm I didn't go to do it, 'm ; and, please 'm, I won't do it never no more," said William Langdale, in a mock piteous tone, whereupon his wife rose from her chair, and gave him a little box of the ears that might possibly have injured a butterfly; and then sailed away to the drawing-room to write for cards to view Mr. Robins' Paradise.

CHAPTER V.

MRS. WILLIAM LANGDALE, being
a woman of considerable decision
of character, and perhaps slightly impatient,
when once she had decided until that
decision could be carried into effect, did
not entrust her note to the post, but
despatched it by the saturnine Perkins.
With a similar promptitude she received
by special messenger on the following morning the requisite order to view Mr. Robin's
river-side Paradise; so, ordering her open
barouche, she drove down after breakfast;

taking with her, a daintily arranged little
lunch, deftly folded in the snowiest and finest
of damask napkins, and laid, like a large
egg, in a jaunty, coquettish-looking basket.
A slender flask of her favourite sherry shared
the basket amicably with the contents
of the napkin, and thus provided for all
contingencies, the fair and gay explorer
set forth with a light heart and a cheery
smile on her voyage of discovery.

Those were not the days when travelling-
gastronomy had reached the dignity of a fine
art. Elaborately arranged luncheon-baskets,
provided with changes of plates and an
armoury of knives, forks and spoons, and
containing also a bewildering choice of fish,
flesh, fowl and pickles had not been invented;
if they had, Mrs. William Langdale would
have been provided with the best that
money could buy, and would have used

them both wisely and well on this and all
similar occasions; for Mrs. William Langdale
was a woman of sagacity and sound
philosophy. She enjoyed her life and all the
good things thereof with a thorough, and yet
most delicate and lady-like enjoyment; she
did not see any reason for interrupting or
foregoing any of those little enjoyments
when a little forethought could avoid any
such interruption. To the " inevitable " she
bowed her head with a grace and a good
temper that was alike charming and philo-
sophic. However disagreeable the position
into which she might be accidentally thrown,
however severe the privation or inconvenience
which it involved, however vulgar or otherwise obnoxious the people with whom it was
necessary for the moment to meet, if the
thing was " inevitable," she encountered it
without the slightest peevishness or vexation

of spirit, and exerted herself womanfully to
make the best of everything and every body.
But it must be confessed that she lacked the
fine spirit of voluntary martyrdom; she did
not glory in life's miseries and discomforts as
she ought to have done; and she was
lamentably deficient in Pelicanism. This,
perhaps, was excusable from the fact that she
had no little "pelicans" for whom to pluck
off her feathers, and therefore, perhaps, it
was not altogether criminal to prefer to
wear them herself, and to add to them, not
infrequently, those of the ostrich and the
marabout. Both of these adornments were
then in fashion; the delicate and humane
modern refinement of wearing the feathers of
our little song birds, plucked from them
whilst still alive (and presumably kicking),
had not yet been adopted by the gentle ladies
of " merrie England."

Born epicurean as she was, and confirmed in this comfortable philosophy by her too indulgent husband, she had yet a warm and tender heart for all who suffered pain or woe, and the glistening tear would start unbidden when the fountains of sympathy were touched by homely sorrows. Nor was it the tear only that fell upon such sorrows, but a golden consolation followed the silvern sympathy, and these diamonds of the first water were not the less bright for being thus fitly set. However, on this sweet refreshing morning of early summer there was no requisition for either the diamonds or the setting. Nature was in her most smiling, jocund mood, and it would have been difficult in all London to have found a spirit more ready to enjoy such a morning than this joyous-hearted lady. Her roomy barouche rolled easily along on its long perch and C

springs, which (unlike their modern sub-
stitutes, the grasshoppers) gave no humming
vibration down the spine. The comparative
freedom of the streets from the fearful
congestions of traffic which characterise
the London of to-day, rendered it possible
to pass then from East to West without
that disturbance of mind consequent upon
the knowledge that you are passing
through a hundred risks, and that at any
moment, by the miscalculation of the eighth
of an inch, both yourself and your carriage
may be crumpled up like an old cocked
hat. All the varied sights and sounds of
a motley city passed before her like a merry
panorama of real life; the broad green
sward of Hyde Park, with its yet undusty
trees, seemed very pleasant to see; the
quaint, many-gabled houses of historic

Kensington, suggested many gay gatherings therein; then these pleasant thoughts gradually passed on to pleasanter as the fresh country air met her on the way, bringing with it the delicate fragrances from fields and village gardens far away; from which, like a privileged thief as it was, it had stolen many sweets, and yet left more behind; soon the calm broad river came shining into view with lazy barges dropping slowly down, or toiling slowly up; with here, a punt moored deftly in a swim, and there a " trim-built wherry " dashing on as fast as tide and two strong watermen could urge it. Anon more wherries,—some, deep laden down to the gunwale with *pater* and *materfamilias,* and all the little *familia;* some, crank and narrow, long, and slight (the imperfectly developed types of the modern "outrigger") were being sent along by three or four oarsmen in each, with varied speed and skill; anon, a small amphibious urchin, who looked as if he had only been breeched yesterday, was struggling like a gallant little Briton to punt over an unwieldy skiff, with a very shaky and in- sufficient oar; next came sailing by a jaunty yacht with snow-white sails, bright bunting, and smart fresh-water sailors, in clean trim, and after this the still more snow-white swans, with flexile necks for ever on the move.

Some such picture as this, only as far pleasanter to the eye as the reality must ever be to the mere description, was painted upon Nature's canvas as Mrs. Langdale stepped out of the French window of the villa she had come to see, on to a lawn of almost miraculous verdure.   The background to this picture was formed by the soft undulating outline of the opposite bank of the bright river, the wooded hills of Richmond, with ivied and ivory houses nestling on the slopes, like jewelled caskets half-concealed in green velvet.

The broad open lawn sloped downward from the house with a rounded bold sweep, that was only just perceptible, and seemed to blend with the waters as they streamed placidly along, being marked only at the extreme verge by a sunken wall of oak, which served the double purpose of protecting the edge of the lawn from the wash of the tides, and deepening the water sufficiently for convenient landing from the boats. A well-appointed boat was moored in its own little picturesque house, up an adjacent creek, and on this fine summer morning had such a tempting suggestion in it, that after Mrs. Langdale had taken her little picnic lunch under the willows, she bade the gardener bring out the wherry. Embarking in this, she took a small voyage of discovery for a mile or two up stream, to refresh her recollections of the immediate neighbourhood. Returning from this impromptu cruise, the lady set herself seriously to criticise the house and its surroundings, and finding to her great satisfaction that the imaginative and eloquent Mr. Robins had not been able to exaggerate its excellencies so much as he had doubtless intended, or as he would have done had he chanced personally to know anything about the place, she called on that flowery gentleman on her return drive, and arranged to take " Lawn Villa " for the season.

Now, in what manner this very commonplace arrangement affected the ultimate fortunes of Mr. Pierce Falconer and Caroline Langdale, I must leave to be narrated at some future time, because other arrangements of terrible national significance were now destined to affect those fortunes still more strongly.

CHAPTER VI.

THINGS near and dear to us, however really small, and comparatively insignificant, have the power of completely shutting out the larger but distant things of national importance; and hence it is that he who chronicles the vicissitudes of his friends, forgets, in large measure, the time in which they lived, and the concurrent events in the outer world of nations; but now these events asserted themselves so loudly, that it was no longer possible to ignore them.

The generation to which my friends belonged had been cursed by the birth of a Destroyer. This baleful monstrosity of creation, this ban-star of the age, did not appear, as of old, in the shape of an enormous dragon, with cavernous jaws, arrowy tongue, daggerlike teeth, deadly, flaming breath. It did not, as of old, fly between the sun and the earth with such a fearful breadth of wing and length of body as to darken the lands over which it passed. No! in outward semblance 'twas a short, fat man, with a weakness for " boots " to which it ultimately gave its name; with a big head something like an apple-pudding flattened at the top and sides, whilst the sallow face looked as if it had been cast in a plaster-of-Paris mould, and had thenceforth remained unmoved and immovable.

Strip this fat sullen fellow of his uniform and his boots and put him into a convict suit and he would have been recognised at once as a very fine specimen of the genus, *murderer*. And so, indeed, he was; metaphorically, like our old friend the dragon, he had cavernous jaws that swallowed up kingdoms and peoples, and money with a quite omnivorous appetite; and very many arrowy tongues, that had the further inconvenience of shooting out deadly things to a very considerable distance; and teeth that were not only like daggers, but swords and bayonets also; and a flaming breath that consumed whole towns and villages with a charming impartiality; vast wings, and a huge tail of armies that darkened the sun with the smoke of battle, and left the foul trail of the serpent wherever they went.

Now this metaphorical dragon had flung itself with irresistible savagery on all the nations of Europe one after another, defiling their women, robbing them of their priceless treasures, and flooding their streets with blood.

But the day of retribution had come; St. George of England came to the rescue, and the monster had been stricken down; but with too tender and too chivalric a hand; "scotched" but not killed. Banished in silken fetters, who could doubt the issue? The faithless man of blood, to whom the death of thousands was mere sport,—a mere gentle, pleasurable excitement that made the game of war better worth playing, broke loose, of course, and Europe, all aghast, gathered its armies in hot haste; but, as usual, left England to do the lion's share of the fighting, and afterwards claimed the lion's share of the glory, and has hated its champion with a very cordial hatred ever since.

However, the fighting was splendidly done.

St. George maimed the dragon once for all this time; cutting off head and tail, clipping its wings, and relegating the fat man, and his boots, and his glory to where his genuis for "battle, murder, and sudden death" had no scope for producing further disasters in the world.

"Further disasters!" At the first thought one is inclined to ask what "further disasters" this instrument of death and the devil could have inflicted?

Into hundreds of thousands of elsewise comfortable homes and honourable families his wars had brought every conceivable abomination of desolation, from the bitter sorrow of separation and bereavement down to the deadliest, ineffaceable, nameless shames inflicted by a brutal soldiery. Every form of writhing agony that the human form can possibly suffer was suffered; not alone by his enemies, but by his own soldiers on the battle fields and in the hospitals. The imagination fails to form any distinct conception—arithmetic itself is powerless to enumerate the hecatcombs of victims thus wantonly and uselessly mutilated, starved, gashed, shattered, frozen, burnt, drowned, suffocated, and otherwise tortured to death.

The blood which was shed in his wars, if gathered into a stream, would have enabled this hero, this sublime conqueror, to wade up to his chin from Moscow back to Paris; and a very suitable mode of retreat this would have been for him, especially if the tediousness of the journey had been enlivened by the spectres of the dead running along the banks to cheer and amuse him with the thrilling music of groans and shrieks, coupled with everlasting curses on his name and fame. Possibly this is only a pleasure de-

ferred; a final crowning triumph, postponed
to another sphere, where it may probably last
much longer than it could have done on earth,
and where, moreover, it will be shared and
enlivened by the company of past and future
conquerors.

But the further disasters that he might have
occasioned weighed heavily in the thoughts,
and created a very reasonable amount of
painful anxiety in the minds of English men
and women during those eventful days pre-
ceding Waterloo. There was a wide-spread
and unpleasantly vivid forecast that the time
had now indeed come when the future destinies
of England were placed upon such a delicate
balance that the " turn of a straw " would
be quite sufficient to decide the up or down
of her future fate; and what the " down "
would mean was equally vivid to the dullest
apprehension. The heel of the conqueror

had been stamped hard " down " on the neck
of every nation in Europe, and his mildly
benevolent intentions had been scrawled in
large letters of blood and flame in every
capital, so that neither England in general,
nor London in particular, were in any doubt
as to the treatment to be expected if the
straw by chance turned the scale the wrong
way. It was difficult to exaggerate the
possible horrors of such a disaster as this;
the sense of it hung in the air, producing
that vague presentiment of evil which sometimes precedes a violent thunderstorm. The
tendency amongst most was not to talk over-
much; and what was said was curt and monosyllabic, and said with somewhat bated breath,
as though the speaker were listening for the
first roar of the cannon. Men went about
their business dreamily and mechanically, with
very little real interest in what they were

doing; like serfs who, whilst they sow the seeds, have scanty hopes of reaping the harvest. Those of the bread-winners who were not metamorphosed into an improvised soldiery, and who had to leave their loved-ones at home each morning to go and do battle for them in the usual inglorious, but very needful way, parted from wife and children and home somewhat wistfully, wondering whether by night-fall either wife, or children, or home might any longer be theirs. Of course this was simply absurd; just as if the French army could take London by assault without having been heard of before hand!

But we must remember that there were no electric telegraphs in those days, and our fat friend in the boots had a wonderful knack of pitching his armies into a city, with very short notice of what he intended to do. Still, there was a good sprinkling of bold and daring spirits (mostly boys and hob-a-de-hoys), who laughed to scorn all such weak presentiments as these, and defied " Old Boney" to do his worst. Midway between these two extremes of timidity and bravery, there was a fair display of dogged quiet courage, both in the militia and the volunteers, which, if it had been put to the trial, might possibly have somewhat astonished their supercilious fellow-soldiers of the line ; and even " Old Boney" himself. It is true, of course, that these two branches of the service would have been more easily beaten than the line, but it is possible that they might have been equally unaware that they *were* beaten and thus have kept on fighting until the conqueror, being tired of beating them, found it more convenient to retire. Emperor de Boots had more than once been annoyed by this cheerful ignorance

on the part of our " regulars," and, from the
very nature of things, one would infer that
the irregulars would be still more ignorant
on such a subject. Be that as it might have
been, or as it may be, certain it was, that a
grand muster-roll of resolute men gathered
at the call of duty and danger, and being of
the old " fighting" race, it may surely be con-
ceded that they would have fought well, and
to the bitter end, for hearths and homes, and
for wives and sweethearts.

Pierce, Gilbert, and myself joined the
volunteers, and urged Sir Geoffrey to do the
same, to avoid the risk of being drawn for the
militia; but he very quietly put aside our
persuasions; he had strained his means to
provide for Gilbert in that way, but cheerfully took the chance of the disagreeable
alternative for himself; and quite as cheer-

fully bore all the *désagrémens* when the unlucky drawing fell upon him ; his wife and
daughters in vain used their utmost en-
treaties that he should purchase exemption
by paying for a substitute, but he simply
laughed off their earnestness and their tears,
and held his own against us all.

Colonel Falconer had, in this supreme
crisis, yielded to his soldier's instinct, and re-
joined the army under Wellington a few days
before Waterloo. He obtained a commission for
Pierce, who rejoiced like a young war-horse at
the long-desired, long-deferred chance of
battle. We gave him a little supper to cele-
brate his transfer from " the reserve " to the
front, at which Sir Geoffrey and Gilbert sang
that grand old war-song of General Wolfe's,
of " Why, Soldiers, why." Not that there
was much "sighing" on *that* evening with us ;

that is the woman's share of war; probably, a much harder share than we men think.

Alack, what sighs and tears, what fearful forecastings and heart-sickening apprehensions came like a deadly blight over the bright homes of England! And after, how many of those homes were darkened and saddened for ever by the shadows of death that followed!

I know there was one loving heart that had felt the deadly chill of parting; one pair of bright eyes that would be weeping more than sleeping for that night, and many nights to come. Pierce knew this, too, far better than I could, for to him her sorrow was like a minor tone of loving sadness mingling with the clarion of hope and the trumpet-call to battle. But the thought of the " loved and left " nerved many a young arm

www.ingramcontent.com/pod-product-compliance
Lightning Source LLC
Chambersburg PA
CBHW020057030726
47498CB00006B/1834